Blood Moon

Thrillers and Tales of

Terror

I0676011

Bryan Cassiday

Bryan Cassiday

Los Angeles

ISBN: 0615318207

Published by Bryan Cassiday

www.BryanCassiday.com

Los Angeles

Printed in the United States of America

blood moon: (also known as *hunter's moon*) the time of the year in October when the hunt lasts through the day into the night.

Contents

Contract Killer

John didn't like any of this. He was tired and he was getting bad vibrations. The only thing he liked was the ocean breeze coming off the shore that was a mile or so to the west.

"I think I'm dying," said Vincent, who was sitting opposite him on the restaurant patio.

John chortled. "Yeah. This heat is murder."

"That's not what I mean."

John gave him a look. Vincent didn't make any sense, John decided.

"How was Vegas?" asked Vincent.

"Great. Like Frank said in the song, it's my kind of town."

"He was talking about Chicago. How'd you get here to LA?"

"I drove." John grimaced. "I hate driving through the desert. So fucking hot. A hundred and ten degrees. There's nothing there."

"That's Vegas, all right—smack dab in the middle of nowhere. All those miles of beautiful neon lighting up the Nevada night sky."

"And six hours, that's too long in a car."
John massaged his sweaty, aching back with his left
hand. He wished Vincent would get down to brass
tacks. John wanted to lie down in bed and rest his
back in his motel room.

"I need you to do a guy." This was said
matter-of-factly. "I may be dying, so I need it done
chop-chop, before my time is up."

They were sitting on the patio of a west side
burger joint, the LA sun above them naked and
ceaseless. There was a blue-and-white striped vinyl
umbrella in the middle of their white-painted metal
table that shielded them from the afternoon
onslaught of sunshine.

The fiftyish Vincent adjusted the black
plastic-framed glasses on his aquiline nose. He was
wearing a black polo shirt with the crimson logo of
a polo player stitched over his heart.

John, just turned forty, wore a tight grey T-
shirt that showed off his barrel chest and muscular
biceps.

"I'm all ears," he said. "Did you say you're
dying?"

"Do you color your hair?"

"Yeah. Sometimes. It's a disguise."

Vincent nodded. "I thought you were too
young to have white hair."

"True. But guys do age rapidly in my line
of work. Let's cut to the chase." Maybe Vincent
didn't want to talk about dying, John decided, or
maybe he had misunderstood Vincent. In any case,
Vincent had deftly sidestepped John's question
about dying.

Instead, Vincent went on, "The white hair looks good on you. With your tan and all."

There was a pause.

John said, "You said on the phone that you had a job lined up for me. Well . . . ?"

"The guy's your job."

"The guy? What guy?"

Two sparrows fought over a piece of a french fry that lay on the terra-cotta patio.

John noticed a teenager who was sitting at a table on the other side of the patio. The close-cropped blond was feeding onion rings to his pet black Labrador Retriever. The Lab sat on his haunches next to the teen, waiting expectantly.

"Can that kid hear us?" John asked Vincent.

Vincent followed John's gaze, said, "No. He's all the way on the other side of the patio."

"I dunno. He was looking over here."

"He was just lookin'."

The teenager now was contentedly munching a hamburger.

"Maybe," muttered John.

"John, don't you have bad dreams about your assignments?" asked Vincent.

"No. I don't remember any of my gigs."

"Nothing?" Vincent looked skeptical.

"I remember how many bullets it takes to whack a guy. Stuff like that. Because I learn from that. But how loud he screamed or did he piss his pants—I don't remember or care."

"You don't remember how loud they screamed." Vincent sniggered.

John's face was expressionless.

"What do you tell your kids about your profession?" asked Vincent.

"I don't have any kids."

"That you know of," said Vincent with a half-smile.

John's face conveyed nothing.

"Why are you asking me so many questions?" he said. "Are you writing a newspaper exposé on me?"

Vincent shook his head, no. "I just want to know what makes you tick. I want to know what kind of a guy I'm hiring."

There was silence between them.

"John, you are in the unenviable position of having a job that no one wants and providing a service that nobody wants except as a last resort," said Vincent.

"I love it when you talk like a professor."

"Do you disagree with me?"

"What? That my job sucks?" John shrugged. His broad, thick-featured face gave away nothing. "It's a rough job. Gigs are few and far between."

"How many people know what you do for a living?"

"Very few."

"Because . . . ?"

"Because it's not something I can brag about."

"Because you provide a service that basically nobody wants or needs."

"Are you calling me a bum?"

"I just want to know why you don't advertise."

"A guy could get busted for what I do."

"Point taken." Vincent paused a beat. "Why would you want such an unpopular, unsung job?"

John didn't know how to answer. "It's not what I wanted. It's what I am." That sounded good to John, though he wasn't sure what it meant.

"Let me put it to you this way. Most of the time you're out of work. Right?"

"Yeah."

"Don't you feel bad when you're out of work?"

"When I feel bad, I go to Vegas."

"How do you impress a girl when you can't tell her what you do for a living?"

John scoffed. "Girls don't care what you do—as long as you have plenty of the green stuff."

Vincent sipped his Coke through a plastic straw. "But it's got to be frustrating to be in a line of work where you get no recognition and most of the time you're out of work. And to top that off, you provide a service that nobody approves of."

"I could care less if they approve of it. Fuck them. If they don't want to hire me, then fuck them again."

"Let me get this straight, John."

"Yeah."

"What you're saying is, you don't like your employers."

"Don't go putting words in my mouth."

"Put it in your own words, then."

"I could do with another Sprite."

"Sure is a cooker of a day, huh?"

Traffic roared by nonstop on Santa Monica Boulevard, sizzling like bacon on a hot griddle. The air reeked of ozone and diesel exhaust from Metro buses.

Tired of waiting for John to reply, drumming a tattoo with his pudgy fingers on the tabletop, Vincent asked, "So what is it?"

"What's what?" John felt himself becoming nettled. He could not understand why Vincent was grilling him with these senseless questions.

"I'll ask you point-blank. Do you like your employers?"

"What's that got to do with anything?" John's mouth felt dry. He cleared his throat. "I'm a businessman. I do what I'm paid to do. I don't allow my personal feelings to interfere with my work."

"You sound angry."

"I'm a professional, Vincent. Professionals don't get angry, they get the job done."

"I sense bitterness in you. And I agree, John. You have every right to be bitter. You have a thankless, dangerous job. You work hard and you get no respect."

"You got that right. And the damn sun is starting to beat down on the back of my neck."

"By all means, move into the shade of the umbrella."

John slid his bottom along the hot circular metal bench out of the sun, wincing at the sudden warmth beneath his pants. "I can't figure you out, Vincent. I thought you had a job lined up for me. That's why I'm here. That's why I left Vegas and drove through the fucking hot desert to be here.

And all I'm getting from you is 'Twenty Questions.'"

"All in due time, John."

"All in due time, what? I like it when you talk like a professor, but now you're sounding like that guy in 'Kung Fu' on TV and I never liked that show because the Confucius stuff goes right over my head."

"Chill out, John. We're doing business."

"I'm OK. It's this damn heat." John wiped his sweaty brow with a paper napkin. He told himself to relax. Sometimes it was like this. Sometimes the negotiations to do the job were more difficult than the job itself.

He tried to breathe deeply and relax himself, but he didn't want to draw Vincent's attention by being too overt about it. It would work against John to allow Vincent to perceive nervousness in a potential contract agent.

John knew all this from experience. He was not new to this game. He also knew, for the same reason, that dealing with Vincent could be difficult.

"I'll ask you again, John, and I want you to be perfectly frank with me. Do you like your employers?"

"Most of 'em I don't even know. I never seen 'em before. We make deals through cutouts. How am I supposed to know some guy I never even met?"

Vincent leaned back to straighten his back, then leaned forward again. "I know these questions may sound pointless, but I'm trying to understand why you do your job." Vincent coughed.

"Because I like sitting in the blistering sun getting burned to a crisp."

Vincent ignored John's sarcasm and went on, "There aren't many guys in your line of work. Why would anyone pick a profession that virtually nobody wants? Such a dangerous, unrewarding profession?"

John thought a moment. "It's like that Greek fable about the frog and the scorpion." John had the sneaking suspicion that this gig wasn't going to be worth his time.

"Edify me."

John looked puzzled. "I don't speak fucking French."

"That means, tell me," explained Vincent.

"Why didn't you say so in the first place?"

"I'm waiting."

"OK. The scorpion wants to get across the river, but he can't swim, so he approaches the frog sitting near him and asks him for a ride across.

"'How do I know you won't kill me with your stinger while I'm swimming?' asks the frog.

"'Because then we'll both drown,' says the scorpion.

"The frog says OK.

"When they're halfway across the river, the scorpion stings the frog.

"'You fool! Why did you do that?' croaks the frog as he's dying. 'Now we're both gonna drown.'

"'I couldn't help myself,' says the scorpion. 'It's my nature.'"

Vincent grunted.

John didn't know how to interpret that reaction.

Vincent said, "Are you saying you do your job no matter whether your employers like your work or not?"

"I'm saying I'm good at my job. I do it well. It's what I do. And that's the only calling card I need."

Vincent coughed. Strands of phlegm rattled in his throat. "Fuck. I think I'm coming down with pneumonia."

"It's this fucking hot desert weather. Almost as bad as Vegas. It's forty degrees at night and ninety-five in the day. That'll make anyone sick."

"Which brings us to this, John." Vincent removed the straw from his Coke and took a sip from the paper cup, feeling the ice cubes bump against his lips cooling them with their gentle nudges. "What happened on your last job?" he asked dryly. "I heard it didn't go down too good. Like the victim survived."

John's heart pumped harder. "How do you know about this?"

"I got it from Bob, the guy who hired you."

John ground his teeth in anger. "That's privileged client info. He shouldn't've told anyone!"

Vincent held his forefinger to his lips and glanced at the teenager eating with his dog. "Tell me quietly, John."

"The target survived the first time. Not the second."

"Not to put too fine a point on it, but you shouldn't have blown it the first time."

"I pulled it off. That's all he paid me to do."

Vincent sighed. "I don't think I could stand living the way you do, John. Getting no recognition for your work. Working your fingers to the bone. Going through life like a ghost, so to speak. The invisible man who provides a service that nobody wants, except as a last resort. No, I couldn't live like that."

Vincent pushed himself away from the table and stretched his arms over his head.

John didn't know what to say. He wasn't asking Vincent to like the way he made his living. What did that have to do with anything? John wondered.

"Does this mean we don't have a deal?" asked John.

Vincent withdrew a crumpled, bulging envelope out of his trouser pocket and slid it across the tabletop to John.

"The money's in there," said Vincent. "There's also a photo of the target in there and all information you need about him." Vincent stood up, coughing. "Shit. I'll need VapoRub tonight. Pneumonia in the middle of July!"

"The job's as good as done," said John. He scoped out the photograph as he withdrew it from the envelope. "Jeez. It's Bob."

"You have no qualms about whacking him? He tried to hit on my girlfriend Alicia."

John looked chagrined. "If I blow away all my employers, how will I make a living?"

"I want you to whack just one."

John flipped through the cash in the envelope and winced. "Hey, there's blood on it."

"Sometimes I cough up blood."

"You ought to have a doctor look at that."

"Do Bob tonight," said Vincent, and coughed again. "I don't know how much longer I have to live."

From his patio seat, the teenage boy, Alex, watched John and Vincent up and leave. His blue eyes on them, he told his dog, "Duke, something bad's gonna happen. Something bad."

He patted Duke's head, his face etched with worry. The dog moaned in agreement.

#

That night, John drove his black Ford Crown Vic to the corner of Third and Maple and waited for Bob, a red-haired plumber with a penchant for the girls, to return from work to his apartment, a two-story cookie-cutter pink stucco affair.

Idly, John wondered if Vincent really was dying. If he was, it regrettably would mean one less client for John, who had few enough clients as it was. In point of fact, with Bob's death, John would have two less cash cows. He felt like he was cutting off his nose to spite his face.

He had the sinking feeling that he was burning his bridges behind him. But that was the life.

In his lap, John held a .22 automatic. What was taking Bob so long? John wondered. Bob should have been here a half hour ago. John shifted restlessly in the driver's seat.

As he waited in the dying heat of the day under a low, washed-out moon, a guy in a navy blue sweatshirt with the hood raised bellied up to the passenger side of the car. He stuck a silenced .22 automatic through the open window and squeezed off three rounds into John's head.

The little bullets rattled around inside John's brain tearing apart the tissue with no place to go. They didn't have the size or the power to exit his skull.

"The name's Pete," said the guy. "Vincent says he doesn't like guys who blow their assignments. He says it's his nature. And, oh, he says Bob was his cutout. Nice to meet you, John." Pete giggled.

The Cheshire Cat

The man from behind reached around the shorter man's neck and drove the K-bar knife upward from that man's chest into the fleshy bottom of his chin through his tongue through his palate and deep into his brain. The shorter man gasped in extremis and blood seeped out of his mouth and that was that.

They were standing in the night on a winding canyon road's shoulder in the Santa Monica Mountains. Only the taller man was standing now and the other crumpled lifeless in the dirt. The living man was wearing black leather gloves. He removed them deliberately and inserted them into his bomber jacket's pockets.

The canyon road unspooled before him, deserted in the faint moonlight that filtered through the purple scrim of a lone cloud that floated aimlessly in the night sky. Shot through with moonlight, the mesquites soughed in the soft breeze.

The man's heartbeat accelerated and adrenaline coursed through his veins as he stood over the corpse and felt the wind caress his face, the spring air redolent of jasmine.

One down, one to go, the man thought.

#

The next night James and Dave met for dinner at Mr. Chow's in Beverly Hills.

"That's what I like about this place," said James.

"It's sure not the food," said Dave, inspecting the menu.

"No," said James, looking around the restaurant. "It's the celebrities. That guy grinning over there with the dreadlocks and the turquoise satin pants is a famous rap singer," he added, nodding to the left.

Dave kept studying his menu.

James chuckled. "Don't even look at that."

Dave looked up, puzzled.

The maitre d' approached their table in a white tuxedo with a peach bow tie. "Welcome to Mr. Chow's, gentlemen. What would you like tonight? Fish, beef, or fowl?"

"Fish," said James.

"I want some chicken chow mein," said Dave.

"You want chicken," said the maitre d'.

"Chicken chow mein."

"Chicken it is," said the maitre d' and strutted off with their menus.

Dave said, "That guy looks like—"

"Wayne Newton," said James. "I know."

"I don't think he understood my order."

"You only get three choices in this place— and you picked the chicken."

"This place costs an arm and a leg and I don't even get a choice of meals?"

"You can watch the celebrities around you. That's what you're paying for."

Dave shook his head. "What's this all about, anyway?"

"I work for the CIA, Dave. That's why I asked you here."

"What's that got to do with me?"

"Don't act all innocent."

"What do you mean by that?"

"What do you mean by that?" James parroted.

"Stop mimicking me," said Dave.

"Let me tell you a story."

Dave looked at James's grey eyes. They reminded him of carp's eyes for some reason. They had no expression that Dave could fathom.

"I don't want to hear a story," said Dave.

The waiter brought a chilled bottle of Perrier and filled Dave's glass. Dave drank from it.

"It's a short story," said James and bided his time till the waiter departed.

A thirty-something woman with a silicone-enhanced bosom in her décolletage walked by their table and smiled at James. James smiled back. She walked away, smiling.

"Hollywood," said James. He watched the waiter pour Perrier into his glass.

"What?" asked Dave.

"Augmentation. It's obvious in her case."

The waiter nodded to them and left.

"Are you ready now for my story?" James asked Dave.

"You called me here just to tell me a story? Let's cut to the chase."

James ignored Dave's outburst. "I was watching *Three Days of the Condor* on cable the other night and they kept showing pictures of the World Trade Center's twin towers. According to the movie, the CIA had an office in one of the towers."

"And after 9/11 the towers are gone. What's your point?"

"Do you realize how much the world has changed since 9/11?"

"What's that got to do with you and me?"

"Don't worry about it."

Dave looked exasperated. "I'm not worried. I'm trying to understand why you invited me here."

"I'm trying to tell you. Look at those men standing over there in the corner. Those guys with the ear buds and the wires trailing down their necks going down under the backs of their jackets. Do you see them?"

Dave craned his neck around to see what James was talking about.

"So?" said Dave.

"Secret Service agents wear ear buds and wires like that."

"Why would the Secret Service be here? They're bodyguards for Chrissake. They're guarding that rap singer you were talking about."

"Very good, Dave. You're very perceptive. But then again, maybe they're working for the Company—like me."

Dave shook his head. "Why? Why would the CIA have so many people here?"

"To keep you from hightailing it."

"Why would the CIA want me? It makes no sense."

"I told you I work for the CIA. I graduated from Camp Peary aka the Farm."

"Are you telling me this restaurant is full of CIA agents?" Dave scoffed. "And all on my account?"

"All I can tell you is I work for the CIA. I can't tell you a whole lot more than that or I'd have to kill you." James chuckled at his joke.

"Very funny. Enough of this."

Dave put his hands on the white tablecloth and made to stand up.

"Don't, Dave."

"Don't what?"

"Don't move."

"Let's talk turkey or I'm outa here."

"Sit down, Dave."

"No. I'm leaving."

"No, you're not leaving."

Dave was about to stand up.

"Sit down," said James, "or I'll kill you." His visage serious.

Dave couldn't help himself. He cracked a smile. "With what?"

"I'm holding a Glock 29 automatic in my lap."

Dave hung fire, thinking. "I don't believe you. Even if you do, you wouldn't use it in this crowded restaurant."

"It's got a silencer."

Dave tensed. He felt his veins constrict, his body chilling. The rock music playing in the background seemed to wax louder, almost deafening him.

"Sit down, Dave."

Dave sat warily.

"So that's what this all about?" he said. "You came here to kill me?"

"What's this country coming to?" asked James. "After 9/11 I don't even recognize this place anymore. You gotta practically strip to fly on a plane nowadays. A porn queen writes a mea culpa about how to make love that earns millions of dollars. Then she goes out and bleeds the silicone out of her breasts. Her way of apologizing for being a porn queen, I guess. What kind of a crazy world is this, Dave? College kids routinely commit mass murders on campuses. It happens so often these days, it's not even worthy of a headline anymore."

"Just shoot me and get it over with. Anything so I don't have to listen to you ranting and raving."

"You're a funny man, Dave. Let me ask you this. Have you ever heard of waterboarding?"

Dave searched James's face. "I heard about it on TV."

"Yes. The CIA uses waterboarding when they interrogate certain prisoners, like al Qaeda terrorists."

"I heard about that," said Dave sotto voce, looking away from James.

"It's considered torture by some."

"I don't know."

"You don't know what it is?"

"Not exactly."

"It's simulated drowning. Here's one way of doing it. You tie a man down on his back on a board—"

"Why are you telling me this?" Dave interrupted.

James ignored him and went on, "Then you cover his face with a burlap bag and pour water continually on the bag. The victim experiences the sensation of drowning. If you pour the water over his face long enough, he actually does drown."

"If you say so. I don't know."

"But you do know, Dave."

"How would I know?"

"Because you did it." James leaned closer to Dave. "Because you work for the Company just like me. You waterboarded an al Qaeda terrorist, but you went too far and ended up drowning him."

Dave sniggered. "I work for the CIA. Now you're really losing it. You come in here telling me you're a CIA agent and that I'm surrounded by a room full of CIA agents—and now you tell me *I'm* a CIA agent, to boot. This is laughable."

"That's why I'm here, Dave. To tie up loose ends," James said dryly. "You gotta be taken care of. You know too much. You gotta go down."

"The world's not insane—you are!" Dave made a motion to rise from the banquette.

"Don't move or I'll kill you now."

Dave kept his seat. "You got the wrong guy. I don't know anything about waterboarding."

"You're the smoking gun. You're going down."

"Why invite me here to kill me? To kill me in front of all these witnesses."

"Did you ever hear the term 'hide in plain sight'? Or did you ever read Poe's 'The Purloined Letter.' They're both riffs on the same idea. Let me jog your memory. In Poe's story someone hides a letter in a wastebasket so nobody will find it."

"What's the connection between that and me?"

"I kill you in a crowded restaurant right under everybody's noses and nobody notices a thing."

"But they *will* notice. I'll scream in pain."

"You won't have time to scream. You'll be dead too fast to scream. I'm a professional. I know where to shoot you so you die in a nanosecond."

"Nobody dies that fast."

"Wanna bet?"

Dave searched James's expressionless grey fish eyes. If anything, they looked more unfathomable than ever.

At last Dave said, "Then do it and get it over with. What's taking you so long?"

"You don't really want me to do it. You're just saying that."

"Just kill me, already. Anything so I don't have to listen to you prattling away."

"You don't mean that. You'd like to live as long as possible."

"Fuck you, you asshole!"

"Hold it down. You don't have much longer to live."

"You keep saying that ad infinitum, ad nauseam."

"This is in effect your last supper."

"I'm leaving here."

"You're leaving here in a coffin."

The veins in Dave's neck throbbed. "You're the most fucked up SOB I ever met."

"Did you ever wonder what the meaning of life is?"

Dave groaned. "A philosophy lesson now."

"Is there any meaning to it? Is there any meaning to your short life?"

"What difference does it make?"

"Exactly. That's the point, don't you see? It makes no difference. One day you're here. The next you're not. The newspaper boy still delivers the paper in the morning. The sun still rises and the birds start chirping at dawn. It doesn't matter one iota whether you live or die."

"All I can say is, Fuck you."

"But my life is meaningful."

"Why, psycho?"

"Because I'm ending your life. By killing you I'm giving myself meaning in an absurd, hostile universe."

"Excuse me, but I haven't the faintest idea what you're talking about."

"You don't have to be polite. It doesn't matter to me if you're polite. I know you don't mean it anyway. Even if I believed you, I wouldn't spare you."

"You got problems, you sick bastard."

"I'm your problem—and I'm not going away."

Dave sighed. "Can't we discuss this like reasonable men?"

"The time for talk is over. Anyway, I don't make the decisions. I just carry 'em out."

"You're making a mistake."

"No, Dave. You *are* the guy they sent me to whack."

The waiter brought two beers. "Heineken and Corona," he said placing them respectively in front of Dave and James.

James spied Dave trying to signal the waiter with his eyes and told the waiter, "Thank you."

The waiter smiled and left.

"That was stupid," James told Dave.

"You're the one who's stupid. This whole thing's stupid. Haven't you thought this out? You'll never get away with it."

James reached for his glass of beer, thought better of it, and checked his left hand as it neared the cold draft brew. "This is my job. This is what I do. You have no idea what you're up against, do you?" He rested his left hand on the tabletop, careful not to touch any utensils, careful to leave no prints.

Dave squirmed in his seat, sweat beading on his face. "I'm up against a raving lunatic."

"You're up against your fate."

Dave wiped a pearl of sweat from his brow with the back of his hand then said urgently, "Think about it, James. Use your brain. All of these people have seen you. They'll ID you if you kill me. You haven't got a prayer of getting away scot-free."

"They won't know you're dead. They pay no heed. They all have their own little problems in their own little worlds."

"Think, man! After I'm dead, the cops'll ask questions. Somebody's bound to remember you."

"Nobody remembers me. Nobody pays me any attention. That's why I work for the Company. I'm the guy nobody ever remembers. Think of me as the Cheshire Cat. You only see me when I'm grinning—and I'm not gonna be grinning when I take you out."

"There are paparazzi camped outside on the sidewalk waiting to bushwhack celebrities. They probably snapped your picture already."

James smiled. "No way. I'm a nobody. Keep your hands above the table," he warned Dave.

"What is the point of this madness?" Dave flung his hands up in exasperation.

"You waterboarded Tariq to death. It's on tape."

"Burn the fucking tape."

"The tape *was* burned. But you're still here. Now I'm gonna burn you."

"I'm not gonna tell anyone. I do that and I implicate myself."

"They all say that." James paused a beat. "Even Rob."

Dave's face registered shock. "Rob? You did Rob?"

"Last night in the hills."

"You bastard." Dave was squirming in his seat.

"You're the last one left. The last man."

"You can't do this."

James looked Dave in the eyes, said, "I can and I am."

"Where does it end? When does the killing stop?"

"It doesn't. It keeps going. It's like life." James evinced a half-smile at the irony of his words, which, as a matter of fact, he did believe.

Wild-eyed, Dave cast around the room to catch a waiter's attention. Dave was facing the wall, so he had to turn his head around to view the restaurant's interior.

James was facing the front door. He always sat with his back against the wall and facing the front door in a restaurant. You never wanted anyone getting the drop on you from behind, he reasoned.

"Don't look over there," he said.

Dave grudgingly turned back to face James.

"Why do you think I took this seat?" James asked Dave.

When James saw that Dave was about to gesture toward a waiter, James whipped his hand up from beneath the table. A newspaper appeared. Sandwiched inside the folded newspaper was a 10 mm Glock 29 subcompact automatic with an Evolution 40 Suppressor.

James fired once. The bullet caught Dave spang between the eyes. He had no time to scream. He slumped to his side but remained sitting upright. There wasn't much blood in the bullet's entrance. He died instantly. There was more blood behind his head along with gouts of gore and skull fragments that slathered the banquette's Indian red leatherette seat-back.

James laid the newspaper and the automatic on the tabletop.

He searched for the shell casing, which the Glock had ejected onto the tablecloth. The spent cartridge had spun around, clinked against the green glass Perrier bottle, and come to a halt. He retrieved it and dropped it into his trouser pocket.

He removed his off-the-rack jacket and laid it on the banquette's seat so it could readily be seen by the waiters.

He snapped up the gun ensconced in the folded newspaper, wedged them under his armpit, and strolled out of the restaurant.

The restaurant personnel paid no heed to him. They knew he would be back to pay his bill. He wouldn't leave without his jacket. Or so they thought.

I Kill for Your Blood

Dirk Kovic gently bent Phoebe's curvaceous white neck and with his hand nudged the coiling blonde locks of her hair away from her neck, baring its white flesh further. The pulsing curvy flesh, like ripe fruit ready for picking, enticed him.

Phoebe's wide cornflower blue eyes dreamy, she moaned through her pink bow lips and acquiesced to his overtures. She tilted her neck toward him, yielding herself to his desire.

He sank his teeth deep into her rhythmically pulsating jugular. She gasped and shuddered, surrendering to his overpowering arms, his overpowering desire.

Kovic felt the hot spurt of her blood as it spouted into his mouth quenching his importunate thirst.

He lusted for her life, even though he was not of her kind. He was one of the undead.

He was known as many things—vampire, ghoul, the Antichrist, the undead, the evil one. To those not undead, he wore evil and menace around him like a midnight mantle.

And yet, Kovic knew, he was not evil. He could not be evil, for he was beyond good and evil, a la Nietzsche, as he had ceased living.

He had eschewed love in the name of knowledge and power.

As much as he had forsaken love, he had not forsaken lust. He needed the hot sensation of a beautiful woman's blood in his mouth streaming down his ever-parched throat slaking his thirst, for a few moments anyway, until his next victim.

The undying thirst for female blood never left him. The feel of her voluptuous body, throbbing with her lifeblood, obsessed him.

And he knew, deep in his dead heart, that women desired to be plucked and destroyed by him, crushed like rose petals with his iron heel, as much as he desired their lives and their destruction.

He sucked Phoebe's blood for a few more minutes, draining her body of its ten pints of blood in no time.

He gazed down at her with his scalding black eyes. She was already dead, her beautiful body slumping lifeless in his arms.

He dropped her in disgust. As a corpse she held no interest for him.

Some of her blood had gotten into his ear. He swabbed his ear out with his pinky and sucked the blood off it.

He picked up his black gym bag, unzipped it, and withdrew a wooden stake and hammer.

He arranged Phoebe's corpse on her back. He aimed the tapered point of the stake at her chest and, hammer in hand, drove the stake into her heart.

Her dead body arched. A result of her nerves, decided Kovic. Blood did not spurt out, for she had none inside her.

He stuffed the hammer back into his gym bag and strutted away.

═══════════════════════════════════

At the top floor of the seven-story CIA building in Langley, Virginia, the director of operations Helmut Scholls sat behind the massive oak desk in his office.

CIA field agent Victor Ward sat across from him.

Scholls, in his late fifties, studied Ward, who was twenty-odd years younger than he, trying to digest what Ward had just told him.

"Could you repeat that, Ward?" Scholls said. "I don't think I heard you right."

"Yes, sir, you did." Ward looked mystified as he granted Scholls's request: "We have reason to believe one of our agents believes he is a vampire."

"A vampire?" Scholls repeated dryly.

Ward knew he sounded like an idiot when he had said this. Nevertheless, he went on, "He's killing off women in LA and draining their bodies of their blood."

Scholls hung fire, staring at Ward. Then, "Why for Chrissake?"

"As I said, we think he believes he's a vampire, so he acts like a vampire."

"Why does he believe he's a vampire?"

"We don't know, sir."

Scholls fiddled with a paperweight of the Statue of Liberty on his desktop. "Do you know who he is?"

"We're pretty sure it's Dirk Kovic."

"Kovic." Scholls furrowed his brow in thought. "Wasn't he the guy who took out two Taliban terrorists trying to sneak into our country a while back?"

"Yep."

Scholls shook his head of grizzled hair. "Obviously the man needs psychological counseling."

"He *was* under deep cover for six months in Afghanistan."

"That could send anyone over the deep end."

Ward nodded. "Should I send him to our Company shrink?"

"No, Ward. It's too late for that."

"But you said—"

"If he has indeed killed these women like you say," Scholls interrupted, "he has to be removed posthaste."

Ward did a double take. "Removed, sir?" he asked warily.

"We have no other alternative," Scholls said, his voice steady. Then he barked, "We can't have a homicidal maniac working for the Agency!"

"Murdering is part of our business."

"But not murdering innocent women. And draining their blood to boot! No, no, Ward. Put an end to this madness pronto."

Ward squirmed in his seat, weathering Scholls's tirade. "How, sir?"

"How?" snapped Scholls.

"How do we remove Kovic?"

Scholls bolted to his feet and walked away from Ward.

"You know what you have to do. Just do it and get it over with," said Scholls, his back to Ward.

"Can't he see a shrink first? The man's one of our best field agents," Ward said, fidgeting.

"No. He's gone rogue. Take care of him."

Still, Ward realized, Scholls wasn't looking at him.

Ward got up to leave. At the door he heard Scholls say, "A friggin' vampire! You gotta be kidding!"

But Scholls still wasn't facing him, and Ward wondered who he was talking to—if anyone.

"Can you imagine if the media ever got wind of this?" Scholls said, gazing out his picture window.

Ward knew it was a rhetorical question so he didn't answer. He edged through the doorway.

Back in his house in the Hollywood Hills, Dirk Kovic thought it was easy for him to pretend to be different people. All of his "life" he had pretended to be alive, impersonating, if you will, a living human being. He was, in effect, always playing someone else.

Therefore, working for the CIA came as second nature to him. The CIA agent's main job, for all intents and purposes, was to pretend to be someone else in order to avoid being unmasked by the enemy.

A vampire, Kovic reasoned, was the perfect recruit for the CIA. No doubt about it.

And on account of their advanced age vampires had acquired vast knowledge in their long life spans. Knowledge, too, came in handy for a CIA agent.

He had amassed knowledge from the likes of Nietzsche, Camus, Schopenhauer, Sartre, George Bernard Shaw, Jean Genet, Tolstoy, the Marquis de Sade, Hegel, Marx, Adam Smith, and a host of others.

Kovic's inquisitive nature was all-powerful. He felt compelled to know everything, and, concomitant with that, to acquire riches as well.

But, of course, what he wanted most, Kovic knew, was human blood, the hot steaming elixir of life, that which was denied him in his own undead body. Especially the blood of young lovely nubile women.

He all but fainted just thinking about it.

In his kitchen he opened his brushed aluminum refrigerator and surveyed serried rows of wine bottles that stood chockfull of blood. He grabbed one of the bottles and swigged the cold blood.

He grimaced. He much preferred the taste of fresh hot blood to cold blood, but, cold or hot, it provided the nourishment he craved.

Dirk Kovic, vampire. It had a nice ring to it, Kovic decided.

How many more of his kind roamed the streets and alleys of LA in the dead of night? he wondered.

―――――――――――――――――――

Scholls and Victor Ward rode in Scholls's black stretch limo to Ronald Reagan Airport.

Ward took a shine to the plush leather seats. He could get used to being rich real fast.

"Do the LA cops know Kovic's killing these women?" asked Scholls.

"Not that I know of. They haven't pulled him in for questioning."

Scholls turned to face Ward and gave him a meaningful stare. "They must never know. If they find out, they'll crucify us."

"They won't."

"By the by, how can you be so sure it's Kovic who's murdering these women?"

Ward hesitated. "We have reason to believe―"

"Cut the crap, Ward. What do we know about Kovic? Girlfriends, boyfriends? What's with this guy?"

Ward shifted uncomfortably in his seat. "No steady girlfriend. There's no reason to believe he's gay."

"What makes you think he believes he's a vampire?"

Ward pulled a *Los Angeles Times* article out of the breast pocket of his beige sports jacket and handed it to Scholls.

Scholls skimmed the article. "Three women have been drained of their blood and left with wooden stakes in their hearts in LA."

"Trademark of a vampire: draining his victim's blood."

"Or someone who thinks he's a vampire."

"Or wants others to think he's a vampire."

Scholls handed the article back to Ward and asked, "But what makes you think Kovic did them?"

Ward shrugged.

"You must have something on him," persisted Scholls.

Ward relented. "He tried to bite one of our female agents in the neck."

Scholls's bushy white foxed eyebrows rose in unison. "Is she OK?"

"Yeah. She fought him off then ran for her life."

Scholls rubbed his brow. "This can't be happening."

Ward sighed. "But it is."

"One thing puzzles me."

"Only one?"

Scholls ignored Ward's black humor. "Why does he hammer stakes through the women's hearts?"

"Because he's nutty as a fruitcake," joked Ward.

"I'm serious. Does he do it after he drains their blood or before?"

Grim-faced, Ward reached into his pocket again, fumbling inside it. He plucked out a black-and-white photo of one of the murder victims.

"We have a contact in the LAPD," he told Scholls by way of explanation.

Scholls scrutinized the photo.

Ward said, "As you can see, there's no blood on the woman's blouse in the chest area."

"So?"

"So her body was drained of blood before the stake was driven into her heart."

"Then what's the point of the stake? Pardon my pun."

Ward's fleeting grin with half his mouth vanished almost as soon as it had appeared. Ward shrugged, as if to say he didn't know.

"Keep all of this between you and me," said Scholls. "You haven't told anyone else about Kovic, have you?"

Scholls tensed up, hunching his shoulders, and bored his beady green eyes into Ward's.

"No," said Ward.

"Are you sure?"

"Yes."

Scholls relaxed back in his seat. "Good."

"Rita knows about it, of course," Ward said.

"Rita? Rita who?"

"Our field agent. The one who was attacked by Kovic."

"All right." Scholls stroked his sharp foxlike chin with his left hand, lost in thought. "Keep everyone else out of the loop."

"What about the guy I get to remove Kovic?"

"There's not gonna be a guy."

"But who's—"

"You're removing Kovic yourself," Scholls chimed in.

"I think we should hire an independent contractor to do it. Those guys are pros. They know how to do it clean."

"No. Listen to me. Tell no one. That's an order, Ward. The fewer people who know, the less chance of a leak."

"What about Rita?"

Scholls mirrored Ward's concern.

"Do you think she told anyone else about Kovic assaulting her?" asked Scholls.

"I doubt it."

"You *doubt* it?"

"It's not the kind of thing you go around telling people."

"Yeah, well, tell her to clam up on this."

"She might have other ideas. She might want therapy."

"Look, Ward. Persuade her to see the light, and don't pull any punches—if you catch my drift."

"I'll do my best."

"That's not good enough. You *will* do it."

Ward bit his words back. He ground his teeth. He was letting Scholls get under his skin. The bastard was good at it, Ward knew.

Scholls turned to him. "That being said, why did—what's her face?—Rita confide in you of all people about Kovic's assault on her in the first place?"

Ward paused a beat. "We're friends. We did a job together."

Changing the subject, Scholls said, "The thing is, he's got his stuff ass backwards. The vampire thing, that is."

"What do you mean, sir?"

"You kill a vampire by hammering a stake through his heart. The vampire doesn't kill his victims with a stake."

"He's certifiable. He doesn't know what the hell he's doing."

"Do you know how to kill a vampire?"

Ward chuckled. He couldn't help himself. "Yeah. But he's no more a vampire than you or me. I'm not gonna need a stake to do him."

Scholls ignored Ward's response. "How do you kill one?"

Ward turned serious. "Like you said, you put a stake through his heart. Everyone knows that."

"Is that the only way?"

"Of course not. You can kill him by exposing him to direct sunlight."

"That it?"

"You can kill him by cutting off his head."

"Hmmm."

"And there's something about running water, too. That's supposed to kill him, I think."

⸻

That night, Kovic couldn't believe how easy it was to lure Rita to his house. You would think she would know better, he decided, after their last encounter.

But then again, no woman could resist a vampire, he knew. Not once he wanted her. And he wanted Rita.

He had to have her. Her ripe neck. Her sheeny crimson blood that coruscated in the moonlight as he sank his hard teeth into the delicate, fragile-like-a-rose flesh of her throat. Her thick blood that gushed into his greedy, eager mouth.

They were standing outside on the balcony of his Mission-style adobe house in the Hollywood Hills, a gentle breeze fondling them. He realized there was a bat perched on the red-tiled roof watching them. It bared its teeth, grinning at them.

He sucked her body dry from the vessel of her throat, his eyes on the full moon as he savored the last drop of her rich, metallic blood.

Bloated with her life juice, he stood there contemplating the moon, licking his blood-splattered lips. If he believed in a god, he would have prayed now, he thought. It was such a mouth-watering feeling standing there satiated with blood and with the power of it that coursed through his undead arteries all the while beholding the icy savagery of the moon above.

He wanted to scream with delight, but he heard the doorbell ring, breaking the spell.

Rita, age thirty-one, is dreaming she's wandering through the dark woods, in a diaphanous white gown.

Her ears prick up as she hears the howling of a pack of wolves.

She hastens her pace through the moonlit forest, hoping to elude the circling baying wolves.

She realizes her feet are bare and sore from the prick of pin needles and debris that litter the ground.

Out of nowhere, mist swirls through the trees. Bats dart from the treetops, diving and swooping. They seem to be zeroing in on her.

She waves her arms, fending the bats off. They snatch at her hair with their razor-sharp rodent teeth. She brushes the bats off her hair with her flailing hands. Crickets chirp. The bats peep. Tree frogs croak. A writhing pack of rats shrieks past her feet. Screaming, she leaps out of their way. The rats surge past her, squealing in unison.

The woods throb with life. And yet . . . the wolves seem to be hemming her in, their circle tightening around her like a noose closing around her neck.

She hears a thundering clamor. The ground shakes under her naked feet. She casts around the forest and sees it. A black carriage, pulled by a team of lathering galloping black stallions, careers toward her.

She hears the brittle crack of a whip. It is him! She sees him. Decked out in a black cape, he stands on the carriage seat's footrest snapping a whip above the frothing horses, his hair streaming in the gusting wind, his black eyes flaming and wild.

He is the Dark One, her knight in black armor, come to rescue her.

#

Victor Ward was driving a rented Crown Vic to Kovic's house. He dialed Rita's number on his cell phone. He had to talk to her ASAP about Kovic.

He knew it was illegal to talk on a cell phone while driving in LA, but he doubted a cop could see him in the darkness. Anyway, this was urgent.

"I'm not home right now. At the sound of the beep—"

Grimacing, Ward hung up.

Fog was rolling in down the hills. He was having difficulty making his way through the dense grey bank.

Squinting, he leaned forward in his seat to get a better view of the winding road up ahead. The Hollywood Hills were just that: hills rife with hairpin turns and switchbacks.

Friggin' cow paths! thought Ward.

What Ward hadn't told Scholls was that he was dating Rita. After all, he didn't think it was any of Scholls's business.

Ward knew that Kovic's attack on Rita had devastated her.

The dense fog misted Ward's windshield. He flipped on the windshield wipers. They hummed busily, whooshing back and forth, beating a rhythmic thrum.

He had yet to confront Kovic about the incident with Rita. Now would be a fine time to do it—right before he shot Kovic dead.

Ward glanced at the silenced .40-caliber Sig Sauer SP2022 ten-round semiautomatic that lay on the passenger seat beside him. He mused that the

Sig Sauer .40, the Mercedes Benz of automatics, which used .40 S&W rounds, would even take out an immortal vampire; blow him, in fact, clear across the floor of his fancy digs.

Ward sniggered. "A vampire!" he said, sarcasm dripping from his lips.

Poor Rita, he thought. He wondered if she would ever recover from Kovic's brutal assault. Only time would tell. His throat tightened at the memory of her trauma.

He spotted Kovic's house through the murky darkness and slowed the Ford Crown Vic, the favorite car of cops.

Fog continued to swirl and billow through the hills, damping the air.

Ward cruised to a halt on the side of the road.

The silenced Sig Sauer made the weapon too bulky to carry in concealment. He turned and reached over to the back seat and snagged his briefcase.

He deposited the briefcase on the passenger seat, opened the lid, and placed the Sig Sauer inside. He snapped the briefcase shut.

Briefcase in hand, he ducked out of the car and made a beeline for Kovic's house.

Reaching it, despite the impenetrable fog, he stood on the front stoop and rang the doorbell. And rang it again.

What was taking Kovic so long? wondered Ward. Was Kovic even home? A light was on inside his spacious silk-stocking house. Where did Kovic get the dough to afford his very own palace?

Ward and Kovic were at the same pay level at the Agency. Ward didn't get it.

He rang the doorbell again, this time holding his finger to the button for at least a good minute and a half.

He thought he heard movement behind the door. He tensed. He felt the adrenaline coursing through his body. He told himself to relax. He didn't want to tip off Kovic to anything untoward.

The door opened an inch, snubbed by a brass chain lock.

"Who is it?" said a disembodied voice.

"It's me, Kovic. Victor Ward."

Fingers undid the chain lock.

The door cracked.

Ward saw Kovic standing there in his foyer looking *content* somehow. Ward couldn't think of another word to describe Kovic. *Content* really wasn't the right word. *Sated*?

Kovic licked his lips.

"Isn't it kind of late for supper?" asked Ward.

"Isn't it kind of late to be knocking on my door in the middle of the night?"

"Sorry about that, Kovic. I just flew in from DC. Scholls sent me to see you."

"Get on with it," Kovic said impatiently.

Ward shivered. "Do you mind if I come in out of this cold fog?"

"I'm rather busy now." He brushed his hair with his hand and cast a suggestive glance into his living room. "Can't this wait till tomorrow?"

"No, it can't. I can never find you during the day. Where do you hang out, anyway?"

Kovic made to close the door in Ward's face. "I really am busy now."

Ward stuck his foot out and blocked the door. "Scholls sent me. Remember him? He's the DO, for Chrissake." Ward added sarcastically, "You know that guy?"

"DO, DC, whatever. Fuck Scholls."

Ward was becoming irritated. "You got something to hide in there?"

"Of course not," said Kovic smoothly.

Ward didn't budge.

Seeing that Ward wasn't leaving, Kovic manifested his vexation. "I told you I'm busy. I'm entertaining, damn it, if you must know. You're such a nerd you can't even take a hint."

"How many times do I have to tell you this is urgent? Your life depends on it."

Kovic heaved a sigh of frustration. "OK. But make it short," he said, opening the door.

Ward entered. "This shouldn't take long."

When Scholls had first given him this assignment, Ward didn't want it. He thought it would be better for all concerned if somebody else, an objective person, namely, handled it. Now, on the other hand, Ward was looking forward to doing Kovic. And why shouldn't he? decided Ward. It was Kovic, after all, who had assaulted Rita.

Ward was going to enjoy wasting the scumbag.

"OK," said Kovic. "What's up?"

Just then a woman walked into the room, or, more accurately, as far as Ward was concerned, she seemed to *glide* in. Ward could see her face from the foyer where he stood with the smug, insufferable Kovic. She was wearing faded blue jeans and a low-cut shocking pink blouse that did little to conceal her ample cleavage.

"Rita!" he called to her.

"Oh, damn," muttered Kovic.

She looked anemic to Ward as she seemed to be floating on air instead of walking.

She approached him, moving spryly on her feet like a cat. "Hello, Victor."

Kovic ordered her to stop.

She halted on a dime.

Taken aback by Kovic's command and Rita's resultant subordination, Ward said, "Don't pay any attention to him, Rita. What are you doing here?"

"I'm thirsty," said Rita, more to herself than to anyone else.

"Go!" thundered Kovic and jabbed his outstretched forefinger toward the living room. "Leave us, Rita."

Ward couldn't take it anymore. He snapped open the briefcase, snatched out the Sig Sauer, dropped the briefcase, and trained the handgun on Kovic.

"Knock it off, Kovic, or I'll shoot."

Kovic seemed to smirk at Ward, which inflamed Ward all the more.

"You're going down," Ward told Kovic. To Rita, Ward said softly, "You can stay, Rita."

Kovic's black eyes smoldered and glowered at both of them.

"I didn't get a chance to finish with you," he told Rita.

To Ward it was inconceivable that Rita was here in the first place. Why would she come back to the very spot where she had been so viciously assaulted?

"You're not going anywhere near her," Ward told Kovic. "Scholls knows all about your antics. You're a flaming nutcase. You think you're Count Dracula or something. You're going around mutilating women and driving stakes through their hearts."

"The stake," said Kovic to himself, ignoring Ward. "I didn't get a chance to put the stake through her heart."

"Then you admit you're a psycho," said Ward.

Kovic glared at Ward for the better part of a minute, but said nothing.

"You shouldn't have messed with Rita," said Ward. "She's mine."

Kovic paused a beat, then guffawed. At last he scoffed, "Yours?"

"She's my girlfriend."

"She wouldn't be yours even if you paid her. You're a three-time loser, Ward. Rita doesn't like losers. She doesn't have sex with losers."

Ward bridled. He wanted to whack Kovic on the spot, but he had to know—

"Why did you put stakes through the hearts of the girls you murdered?" he asked Kovic. "You got the vampire legend all upside down. Vampires are killed *by* stakes. Vampires don't kill *with* them. That's what tipped us off that you're nothing but a basket case."

"Competition," said Kovic without skipping a beat.

Confounded, Ward said, "What kind of cloud-cuckoo-land are you living in?"

"I don't want the competition. My victims will turn into my competitors, fellow vampires, if I don't use a stake on them."

"You got this loony business all figured out, huh?"

"Hence, Rita."

"Leave Rita alone."

"You interrupted me by being here. I didn't have time to finish her off with a stake."

Baffled, Ward could do nothing but shake his head. "What are you babbling about?"

Rita approached Ward, her eyes burning with desire for him—at least that's what it seemed like to Ward.

"Don't you get it?" Kovic asked Ward.

"Would you knock off the bughouse bullshit!"

Rita leaned toward Ward's throat, hungering for him.

"She doesn't want you," said Kovic. "She wants your blood."

"You're a raving lunatic!" cried Ward. "You fuck!"

Ward fired off three rounds pointblank into Kovic's chest. Kovic reeled backward.

Rita buried her teeth up to the hilt into Ward's throat, moaning with ecstasy.

"Oh no!" Ward wailed.

End of the Line

When the stranger came in, Jack Dalton had no idea the guy was going to rob the bank. Maybe the guy's gym bag should have tipped him off.

It was closing time and Dalton and another cashier, Tabby, whose last name he didn't know, were the only ones left in the bank, preparing to lock up and go home.

"I had another TB interview last night," Tabby told him.

"TB?"

She had an alluring symmetrical face under her full blonde hair, but her sharp vulpine chin and downturned pouting lips lent her face a mean cast. Dalton figured she must be in her late twenties.

"Too Bosomy," she said. "A modeling interview."

"I never knew you were a model."

"I'm trying to be one but the Hollywood muck-a-mucks keep telling me I'm too bosomy. They say I distract potential customers from the product I'm selling."

"Paying your dues."

"All my life—for nothin'." She sighed.

"You and who else."

"You look like you could be an actor."

"I love you too."

"No. I meant it as a compliment. You're nice and tall."

"It sure doesn't look like I'm gonna be bank president any time soon. I've been slaving here for ten years. And here I am thirty-three."

The guy stepped up to their counter and plunked his gym bag down on it. He had long scraggly hair that spilled over his ears in unruly locks. He wore a yellow Windbreaker zipped over his paunch. Dalton pegged him for a construction worker who just got off duty.

The guy unzipped the gym bag, withdrew a 9 mm Beretta automatic, and trained it on Dalton's face, changing Dalton's mind about the guy's occupation.

"Give me the keys," the guy demanded.

"What keys?" asked Dalton.

"To the front door."

Dalton reached under the counter, retrieved the keys from the hook they hung on, and dropped them on the counter.

The robber snagged the keys, ran to the front plate-glass door, locked it, and drew the venetian blinds shut. Then he sprang over to the back door and locked it.

While the guy was busy locking up, Dalton stepped on the red plastic button mounted in the floor that signaled the cops that a robbery was in progress. His heart in his mouth, he wondered how long it would take them to get here.

He noticed that Tabby looked like she was about to faint. Her face was so white it all but glowed.

As the robber returned to the counter, the bank guard walked out of the men's room, picked up on the robber's gun, and went for his. Without batting an eye the robber shot the guard on the spot. Once in the head and once in the chest.

The guard fell backward onto a desk and seemed to sit there as if meditating. The only thing that destroyed the illusion was the missing chunk of skull that had been blown off the right side of his blood-soaked face.

Annoyed that the guard continued to sit on the desk as if alive, the robber stalked up to him and shoved him with his free hand. The guard fell over backwards onto the desktop.

Cursing, the robber bolted back to the counter.

Dalton didn't like the look of the guy's eyes, which seemed to be popping out of their sockets.

"It's rising," said the robber. "I know it's rising."

"What's rising?" asked Dalton.

For all answer the robber dug into his gym bag and fished out a black cuff of some kind.

"My sphygmomanometer," the robber muttered to himself. "Never leave home without it."

"Sphyg—" Tabby said, puzzled and unable to pronounce the word.

"A fucking sygno-, spig—hell, now I can't pronounce it either. It's a blood pressure cuff."

He wrapped the cuff around his arm, secured the Velcro band, and pumped air into the inflatable rubber cuff.

Reading the gauge he deflated the cuff, said, "Too high. One eighty-five over one forty. Godddamn! And I'm all out of Monopril. My head's gonna explode." He repeated *explode* and laughed maniacally as if he had said something hysterical.

At loose ends, for lack of anything else to say, Dalton asked, "What's the pressure supposed to be?" Maybe the guy wouldn't kill them if they could keep him talking, Dalton decided. *That's right*, he thought. *Humor him.*

"One twenty over eighty. I need money so I can buy medicine. It costs an arm and a leg."

Dalton heard a metallic rattling and turned toward the sound, as did Tabby and the robber. Somebody was trying to open the locked front door. Dalton couldn't see who it was. Whoever it was gave up and left.

"See. Nobody's gonna save you," the robber told Dalton. "I got laid off from my security guard job and I need money fast." He waved the automatic at Dalton's face. "Don't think I won't use this."

Dalton glanced at the dead bank guard. "Take it easy. Remember your blood pressure." *Stall for time*, thought Dalton.

"Shut up! Open your till and dump the money on the counter."

"Calm down."

"Fuck you, calm down! Tell me to calm down one more time and I'll calm you down by fucking blowing you away."

The robber reached over the counter, grabbed Dalton's head by the hair, put down his gun, and wrapped the blood pressure cuff around Dalton's neck. His mouth a rictus, the robber pumped air into the cuff, which inflated, choking Dalton, whose face swelled and turned red.

"That's what my head feels like, dickhead!" spat the robber, pumping more air into the bulging cuff.

"Stop it!" screamed Tabby. "You'll kill him!"

"If he doesn't open the till, I'll strangle him with this thing."

"OK," Dalton managed to splutter, all but incapable of moving his jaw to talk on account of the inflating cuff pressing beneath it.

The robber deflated the cuff. Dalton coughed and set to breathing again. Dizzy, on the verge of blacking out, he fumbled for the keys and unlocked the till in front of him, rushing it, apprehensive of fainting.

"Don't jerk me around anymore," warned the robber.

"What did we ever do to you?" asked Tabby, her eyes welling.

"You open your till and shut up!" The robber trained the Beretta on her. "I just want the money. This has nothing to do with you."

Dalton tossed packets of twenties on the counter. He blinked his eyes, feeling the excess blood drain from his suffused face.

The three of them started at the sudden strident buzzing of the phone on the counter. The phone demanded to be answered.

The robber looked at the phone, bewildered for a moment.

On the third ring he said, "Who the hell is it?"

"How should I know?" said Dalton.

"Answer it. Act normal."

Dalton lifted the beige plastic handset. "Hello. First Bank of California."

"This is the LAPD," said a man's toneless voice. "We're responding to your alarm. Are you being robbed?"

"Yes," said Dalton as calmly as he could under the circumstances.

"Let me talk to the robber."

Dalton offered the handset to him. "It's for you."

"Me? Nobody knows I'm here." Incredulously he said, "Hello," into the transmitter as he grabbed it.

"This is the LAPD," said the voice. "The bank is surrounded. Come out with your hands up."

"In a pig's eye."

"There's no way you can escape. Do you have a gun?"

"Is the Pope Catholic, tough guy?"

"I take it that means yes."

"Yeah, fucking airhead atheist! What do you think it means?" The robber rolled his eyes in disgust. To Dalton he said, "Where do they get these blockheads?"

"Now look, do you want to do this the easy way or the hard way?" asked the monotonic cop voice.

"No. You look. I'm walking out of here with two hostages and a loaded Beretta in my hand. Got that! Or do you want me to FedEx you a Polaroid of our happy trio?" Exasperated, the robber made a motion to hang up the phone.

"Cool off. Take three deep breaths and think about what you're about to do. There's no way you can escape."

"I'm calling the shots, bonehead. Don't you understand English? What are you? One of those affirmative action atheists they got down there? Yeah, I used to be a cop. One of you fucks took my job. Fucking affirmative action atheists. How does that grab you?"

"All I'm asking you is to think carefully about what you're doing."

The robber's eyes bugged even further out of his head. "And I'm telling you, don't fuck with me or I start whackin' hostages."

He slammed the handset down into its cradle.

"What do we do now?" asked Dalton.

"Those LAPD bums fired me, said I was too stressed out to work. *Said I had a drinking problem.*"

Working his jaw, grinding his teeth, the florid-faced robber winced and clutched his heart, dropping his automatic. To Dalton's amazement, the guy's whole body became rigid as he dropped to the floor.

Circumspectly, Dalton came out from behind the counter and scoped out the motionless robber. He looked dead, decided Dalton. Still wary, Dalton felt for a pulse in the robber's neck.

"Must've had a heart attack," he told Tabby. "No pulse."

"Jeez!" she gasped. "I almost had one myself."

"We better let the cops know we're all right."

Tabby gazed down at the piles of cash on the counter.

As Dalton headed for the front door, she said, "Wait a minute."

"What?"

"Let's think about this."

"What's to think about?"

"Aren't you sick of working for peanuts and getting nowhere fast?"

"What's that got to do with anything?"

"Look at all this cash here." She ogled it, then eyed him. "I know I'm sick of going to modeling interviews and getting rejected day in, day out. 'Oh, Tabby sweetie, you've put on too much weight,' say the casting agents."

"What—"

"That's Hollywood-speak for getting breast implants. I never had an implant in my life. Those cokeheads are so phony they don't even know the real thing when they clap eyes on it."

He headed back to her from the still-locked front door. "Yeah, this is another dead-end job for me too."

"Here's our once-in-a-lifetime chance. Don't you see?"

"If you're saying we should rip off this money, the cops'll nail us."

"Not if we do it right."

"I'm listening," said Dalton.

"The cops don't know the robber's dead. Right?"

"So?"

So she told him.

#

He liked her idea. Full of originality and panache, it all hinged on the cops' believing that the robber was still alive. And he admired Tabby's presence of mind in this tense situation. She had looks women would kill for and a brain to boot.

When opportunity knocks . . . , he thought.

Dalton opened the robber's gym bag. It was empty save for a black plastic rectangular object.

"What's that gizmo?" asked Tabby as he pulled it out.

"It looks like a transmitter of some sort."

She took it from him and was about to push a button on it when he said, "Don't."

"Why not?"

"Maybe this guy has cohorts. That looks like some kind of signaling device."

"OK. Let's take it with us anyway."

They stuffed bundles of cash into the gym bag.

Dallton said, "The beauty of your idea is that the cops'll blame the robber for taking the money and we'll get away scot-free."

"You got it."

The phone rang.

Dalton dropped the cash he was holding, his hair on end. "Must be the cops."

"Crap. What do we do?"

Dalton turned over ideas like a shot. "If we don't answer it, they'll be suspicious."

"Then they might charge in here, and there goes our dough."

"We have to answer it."

"They'll want to talk to the robber."

Worried that the cops would hang up, Dalton picked up the handset on the fifth ring. "Hello."

"This is the LAPD. Give me the robber."

Dalton broke into a cold sweat. Thinking fast he said, "I can't."

"What happened?" asked the cop suspiciously.

"He refuses to talk to you."

"Why?"

"He's shaking his head at me, motioning for me to hang up."

"Tell him we want to cut a deal."

"They want to cut a deal," said Dalton as if he was talking to the robber. To the cops Dalton said, "No. He's shaking his head. He's grabbing the receiver—"

Dalton banged the handset into its cradle.

"We have to get the lead out," he told Tabby.

They stuffed money into their shirts and into their pockets after they had filled the gym bag with greenbacks. Then they tossed cash into canvas money bags that the bank used to transport the cash in armored cars.

"Where's the guy's car?" asked Tabby.

"I saw him come in the front door. It must be out front. He wouldn't park it far away."

Dalton dug the guy's keys out of his trouser pocket. The key tag in the shape of an eight ball had the car's license plate number printed on it in white letters.

"2 Z DETH," he read out loud. "Should be easy to spot."

"I didn't hear you."

"It's a vanity plate—"

To his horror he heard the phone commence ringing.

"Oh no," said Tabby.

"I'm not answering it. Let's split."

They bent over and lifted the robber.

Tabby groaned. "He weighs a ton. Why does his stomach feel so hard?"

"He likes you."

"Very funny," she said, not meaning it.

"It feels like a flak jacket. He really came prepared for a shootout."

Dalton draped the robber's left arm around his neck.

"You hold him while I put the gun in his hand," said Tabby, retrieving the Beretta from the floor.

She placed the automatic in the robber's hand. The phone kept ringing as if angry that nobody was answering it, driving Dalton nuts.

"We have to get out of here," he said.

"The gun won't stay in his hand," she said in frustration, trying to fit the butt into the robber's motionless hand.

"Give me the gun."

She handed it to him and he said, "I'll hold it and make believe my arm is his arm."

He wrapped his right arm around the robber's waist and leveled the Beretta at himself.

"I'll carry the money bags," said Tabby. "I wish that damn phone would shut up."

"Press against his side so nobody can see his right arm."

Lurching, they made for the front door.

Dalton slipped on the guard's blood that was pooling near the desk. He stumbled and would have fallen, had not Tabby steadied him and the robber.

Ten-odd feet from the door Dalton felt pressure around the nape of his neck.

"What are you doing?" he said.

"Nothing," said Tabby.

"You're hurting my neck. Stop it!"

"I'm not doing anything."

"Christ! He's still alive. He's trying to strangle me."

"Are you kidding? That's not funny."

The phone seemed to be ringing louder and he had trouble discerning her words. Feeling for a seam in the robber's flak jacket, he squeezed the Beretta's trigger, aiming at the seam, and pumped a round into the robber's chest.

Dalton felt the pressure around his neck subside.

Tabby jumped at the crack of the automatic's firing, then looked at Dalton and said, "That was cool. You're totally cool."

"We gotta do whatever it takes to hold onto our money—just like the rich guys."

"Right. He would've grabbed our money for himself."

Dalton noticed that the phone had ceased ringing. "The cops must've heard the gunshot. It's now or never," he added, making a move toward the front door.

"You forgot something," she said, pulling to a halt.

"We don't have time for it. The cops could rush the bank any second. Let's get cracking." He tried to step forward but she wouldn't budge, holding her ground just out of reach of the front door.

"You forgot," she said.

"What?" he snapped.

"His eyes are closed. The cops'll spot right away that something's wrong."

Dalton racked his brains for a solution. "What about shades? Do you have any?"

"Yeah, in my purse."

She had to put a money bag down to delve into her purse and fetch her sunglasses. She slid their pink plastic bows over the robber's ears. She lifted the money bag and helped Dalton haul the robber to the door.

She unlocked it and they trudged onto the sun-gilt sidewalk. Two black-and-white squad cars, their red, white, and blue light bars flashing, were parallel-parked across the street.

Four cops that Dalton could see were hiding behind the squad cars, their service revolvers braced on the hoods of their cars, drawing beads on the robber. There could be a sniper lying in wait somewhere high above, for all Dalton knew.

He set eyes on the robber's banged-up Dodge, which was parked in front of them.

Hoping the cops would hold their fire Dalton guided the robber toward the car and trained the Beretta on his own chest, expecting the cops to twig the gun. He figured the sight of the gun would deter them from shooting lest the robber plug a hostage in retaliation.

So far so good, decided Dalton.

There was no traffic on the street, Dalton realized. That would work in his and Tabby's favor. No traffic to impede their escape. The cops had barricaded the street directly in front of the bank.

Dalton made the driver's side door. It wasn't locked. Tabby opened it and now they would have to become acrobats to slip inside.

"Give it up!" boomed a police bullhorn. "Stop here and nobody gets hurt!"

Tabby slid across the front seat to the passenger side and helped pull the robber in beside her. Dalton's back was killing him. The robber's legs got wedged in the doorway and held up the proceedings. Dalton couldn't lean over and pull up the guy's legs because that would look untoward to the cops and they might think something was up.

"Pull his legs in," he urged Tabby. "They're stuck.

Tabby leaned forward into the driver's side footwell and tried to haul the robber's legs in. They wouldn't budge. Then she yanked on his trouser leg, jockeyed it, and at length freed the wedged leg. The other one followed suit.

Dalton slipped in beside the robber onto the front seat and closed the door. They were all set, decided Dalton.

"Talk to us!" bellowed the grizzle-haired tall cop with the loudhailer as he stood behind a squad car.

Dalton cranked down the window and yelled at the cop, "He wants you to leave us alone or he'll shoot me!"

The cop looked puzzled. "Can't he speak for himself?"

Dalton turned his head toward the robber and mimicked talking to him. Think, Dalton! he told himself. He faced the cop again.

"He says you'll ID his voice with a voice print if he talks," said Dalton.

The cop shrugged it off, unable to account for the whims of crooks. "Throw down the gun and come out of the car," he announced through the loudhailer.

Dalton inserted the key in the ignition and fired the engine. He pulled out onto the street, keeping sight of the cops. He glanced in the rearview mirror. A squad car was giving chase, its light bar flashing.

"We've got company," said Dalton.

"You'll have to lose him," said Tabby, peeking back over her shoulder at the squad car.

"Easier said than done."

"I'm not a hooker," said Tabby, apropos of nothing.

Dalton peered through the windshield, trying to figure out where to go. Left? Right? Where? he wondered.

"I am *not* a hooker," repeated Tabby. "I'm a model."

He had no idea what she was talking about.

"I am *not* a cashier anymore," he said, a lopsided grin on his face.

"You were cool back there."

"I have a confession to make."

"Don't tell me you're a cop." She studied his face. "I told you I'm not a hooker."

"No way am I a cop."

"Then what?"

"I never killed anyone before."

"You could have fooled me."

He paused a beat. "I never knew it was so easy."

Tabby punched the cadaver in the chest. "Ouch! You didn't have any choice. The SOB wanted to steal our money. He deserved to be shot."

Dalton drove down Wilshire Boulevard, three squad cars in tow now, the traffic sparse. The cops must have put out the word for motorists to stay off the street.

"The problem is, how do we ditch those cops?" he said.

He heard a whirring sound overhead and knew without having to look that a chopper was hovering over the car.

"Especially with that chopper tracking us," she said.

He drove up the on-ramp of the 405 Freeway, heading south, then bore west on the 10.

"We'll be on TV tonight," he said.

"We may already be on it," she said, looking up into the sky.

He followed her gaze and caught sight of two choppers floating like evil grasshoppers in the clear sky.

"Where are you going?" she asked.

Dalton shrugged. "To the beach, I guess."

"We've got to do anything to protect our money, Jack. I don't want to go back to being rejected at job interviews for the rest of my life. I'll lose my mind."

"What's that noise?"

A beeping sound was emanating from the gym bag. Tabby unzipped it and saw a red light flashing on the robber's transmitting device.

"This gizmo's beeping," she said, withdrawing it from the gym bag.

"Do you hear that?"

"The beeping?"

"No. Another sound. Listen. Something's buzzing."

She held the transmitter to her ear. "It's not this. This is just beeping."

"It sounds like it's in that guy's Windbreaker."

She unzipped the Windbreaker and gasped. "Uh-oh."

"What is it? I can't see."

"It's another gizmo with a flashing red light on it and wires leading from it."

"Where do the wires go?"

Tabby opened the jacket wider and traced one of the wires. "Shit!"

"What the hell is it?" asked Dalton, starting in his seat as she yelled.

"It's . . . it's dynamite. Sticks of dynamite are sewn into this flack jacket. We're gonna blow up!"

Dalton saw the McClure Tunnel coming up fast in front of him.

"All right, all right," he muttered, though it well and truly wasn't all right, not in the least.

"He's a walking time bomb!"

"He wasn't kidding when he said his head was gonna explode."

"How can you crack jokes at a time like this?"

"I'm stopping under that tunnel. Then we bug out. Got it?"

"Yeah. Can't you go any faster?"

The buzzing and beeping of the devices were accelerating, fraying Dalton's strung-out nerves.

"The choppers can't see us when we abandon the car in the tunnel," he said. "That's when we make our getaway."

He slammed on the brakes in the tunnel and he and Tabby hauled the money bags out of the car on the spot. Squinting, he sprinted with her toward the freeway's shoulder in the dark, aided only by the faint light diffusing from the sodium-vapor lamps in the tunnel.

The first squad car, its driver caught off guard by the Dodge's sudden stopping and by the darkness of the tunnel, plowed into the Dodge's rear bumper.   Seconds later, the Dodge exploded, flooding the tunnel with flames and billowing black smoke.

The deafening eruption knocked Dalton and Tabby to the ground, their ears roaring. Choking on the smoke, they staggered to their feet and made for the tunnel's beach-side exit.

Through the screen of swirling smoke Dalton discerned an approaching car and waved it down. The driver stopped, though he was having difficulty making out Dalton through the dense banks of smoke mushrooming out of the tunnel's opening.

Dalton saw that the man was driving a Mustang convertible, its top down. Dalton opened the driver's side door, pulled out the Beretta from his waistband, and shot the middle-aged driver point-blank in the forehead. Dalton dragged him out of the Mustang and dumped him on the road.

Then he shot the man's hysterical bottle-blonde wife twice in the head, which blew up and splattered the window on her right with blood and brain matter, and cut off her screams in her throat, as well.

"Get in," he told Tabby. He flung the money bags into the back seat of the Mustang.

She gazed at him with saucer eyes. "Wow," was all she said.

"Get in."

"Why'd you kill them?" She had trouble hauling the dead blonde out of the car.

Giving the blonde a push to help Tabby as he settled into the driver's seat, he said, "Witnesses."

Tabby dropped the woman on the street and groaned with the effort.

"What's gotten in to you?" she asked, her blue eyes locked on his. She slid into the car beside him.

"If we left them alive they would have ID'ed us. And . . ."

"And what?"

"And the fire will burn their dead bodies. The cops'll think we're the ones who are dead."

"I never thought of that," she said, gagging on the smoke clouding over the car. "I'm suffocating."

Dalton put the brand-new silver Mustang GT convertible in gear, pulled a U-turn, and drove out of the tunnel toward the beach.

"Roll down your window," he told Tabby. "There's blood on it."

"OK, Joe Cool."

"I like this car."

"We're moving up in the world, all right," she said, smiling, basking for a moment in the brackish onshore sea breeze that caressed her face.

"You better believe it," said Dalton, enjoying the breeze likewise.

"Now pull over," she said, her voice hard.

"What? We've gotta get out of here. The cops—"

"Pull over, I said." She jammed the automatic's muzzle into his rib cage.

Shocked, he could do nothing but stare at her in awed disbelief. "What's gotten into you?"

"End of the line for you, Jack." She jabbed his flank with the gun barrel again.

There was nothing for it. Dalton pulled over onto the dirt shoulder. The Mustang's eighteen-inch tires crunched the dirt and gravel beneath them as he tooled to a stop.

"Now what?" he said.

"Get out," she said, training the automatic on his face.

Grudgingly, Dalton climbed out of the car.

Tabby slid into the driver's seat. She held the gun steady on him all the while.

"I don't get it," he said.

"That's your problem, Jack. You just don't get it. You'll never get it."

He stood there and watched her drive up the winding Coast Highway, a couple of desolate, fraying clouds dawdling in the sky above her. The sun languished in a corner of the sky, mute.

She waved to him with the back of her hand.

"Bitch," he said under his breath.

Among Us

I should have known something was wrong when I noticed that my next-door neighbor Tom Foley wasn't outside that Sunday morning washing his silver SUV.

He was regular as clockwork washing that car every Sunday, even in the rain.

I did not give it much thought and drove my '71 VW Bug to Herb's gas station about a mile from my crib.

Herb, in his early thirties with a flaming red beard worthy of a Viking, stood in the doorway of his gas station's office and yawned when I pulled up to him.

"Didn't get enough sleep last night, Herb?" I asked.

"I don't have time for sleep."

"Maybe you should make time."

"I got too much work to do, Ernie. You fuckin' artsy-fartsy painters. What do you know about a little old-fashioned work?"

"Very funny."

"When did you get back from your vacation?"

"Last night."

Herb yawned again, his bloodshot blue eyes watery.

I got out of my Bug.

"You look like you could do with a vacation, Herb."

"No time. No way."

I shook my head in wonder. "Is this the new Herb? Are you reinventing yourself?"

"What are you talking about?"

"Not long ago, you used to go fishing up at the lake every chance you got."

"Like I said, no time for that."

"All work and no play . . ."

"Let it die, Ernie. Want some gas or not?"

As I walked toward the pump, I spotted a man smoking a cigarette in his car as fuel pumped into his gas tank.

"What's that idiot doing?" I asked Herb.

"That's old Sam Hodges," he told me. Then he called to Hodges, "Put out that damn cigarette when you're pumping gas, Sam!"

Sam paid no attention to him, went right on smoking.

"I tell you, people in Aldamo are acting weird lately," I told Herb.

At that moment a black four-wheel-drive SUV pulled away from a pump near Sam's. As the car sped away, I could see that the gas nozzle was still stuck in the car's tank.

The car accelerated, kicking up dirt and gravel. The rubber gas hose stretched as far as it could go. All of a sudden, the steel nozzle shot out of the car's gas tank and snapped back into Sam's windshield.

The windshield fractured on impact. The gas-spewing nozzle slammed into Sam's face. His burning cigarette ignited the gas fumes. Sam's car burst into flames, as well as did Sam. His face looked for all the world like a wax dummy's melting.

"What the hell's going on!" I cried.

Herb stood dumfounded, looking on.

There was no time to help poor Sam. Before we could make a move in his direction, his fiery car exploded.

Herb and I dove away from the flames as they engulfed the gas pumps, which triggered another explosion, much louder than the first.

"How many fools we got in this town?" I said, my ears ringing, as I lay on the ground. I coughed on the dust my dive had raised. "What's going on, Herb?"

Herb was nonplussed. His livelihood was going up in flames before his very eyes.

At last he muttered, "I never liked that guy anyway." He trudged toward his office, shoulders slumped. "I'm ruined."

"At least we're still alive," I called after him.

"I'm nothing without my job. I might as well be dead."

He shambled away from the flaming gas pumps toward his office.

"Your insurance will cover the loss!" I hollered above the roaring fire.

I thought I heard him say, "I'm nothing without my job."

He disappeared into his office, only to return three minutes later, a revolver in his hand.

"My life's over without my work," he said, brandishing the firearm.

What was he going to do with that gun? I wondered. It looked like he was waving it at me. Hodges was already dead. Herb couldn't kill him twice. That left me. What had gotten into Herb?

I looked for cover. Frantically, I quartered the area. It was too dangerous to hide behind a gas pump. A stray shot by Herb could ignite another pump with devastating consequences.

Before I could budge, Herb put the gun to his own head.

"It's just a job!" I yelled. "It's not your life!"

He ignored me, pulled the trigger, and blew his brains out.

I stood there in disbelief, as his body crumpled. The wind freshened and changed direction, as if an offshore Santa Ana wind had sprung up out of nowhere, and a bank of black smoke from the burning gasoline wafted over his body, obscuring him. Billowing over the office, the smoke seemed to consume it.

I made for the phone booth at the side of the road and entered it. Inside, I watched the smoke plume over the chaparral that blanketed the valley.

I dialed 9-1-1 and told the police about the accident.

Then I drove my Bug to Dr. Corvalis's house at the other end of the valley.

I had known Corvalis my entire life. It was he who had brought me into the world. He was in his sixties now. Even so, he had not lost the spring in his step or the twinkle in his blue eyes.

I needed someone to confide in. As far as I was concerned, something strange was going on in Aldama. I needed to know if anyone else felt the same way.

I parked my Bug on his asphalt driveway.

He owned a typical Southern California mission-style house, what with the orange pantiled roof and the black-grilled windows. It wasn't ostentatious—Corvalis didn't flaunt his wealth—but it was obvious from its ranchlike spaciousness that its owner had money.

I rang his doorbell.

Since it was Sunday, he should be home.

I was right. He answered on the second ring.

He was glad to see me, almost as glad as I was to see him.

"Long time no see," he said.

"I haven't needed your services lately."

"Thank goodness for that. Knock on wood." He knocked on the door jamb with his knuckles.

"Up until now," I said.

Worry crossed his bearded face for a nanosecond. "You're sick, Ernest? Is that what this visit is about?"

"No, Doc."

He looked relieved. "How's the art business? Selling any of your pictures lately?"

"No. I still need to sell leather goods that I craft to pay the rent."

Corvalis sighed. "That's a shame. But I'm sure it's just a matter of time before your work catches on with the public." His pale blue eyes glinted merrily behind his wire-rim spectacles.

"I need to share my thoughts with you."

"Oh, I'm being rude. Come inside and have a seat."

I did so and sat on a chaise longue in his capacious living room. I tried to sit down, that is, but I could not stay seated. I had to get up and pace around to bleed off the stress that had built up inside me since the inconceivable tragedy at Herb's gas station.

I told Corvalis about it.

His face registered shock. "Can I be of any help to Herb?"

I shook my head. "Half his head disintegrated."

"Why did he take the accident so hard, I wonder?"

"You took the words right out of my mouth. That's why I came here to talk to you."

"What do you mean?" He angled to a sideboard and lifted a bottle of Zinfandel off it. "Care for a drink?"

"All right."

He poured me a glass of the wine and handed it to me.

"Thanks," I said. "What's been bothering me ever since I came back from Mexico—"

"Tijuana?"

"Yeah. Anyway, it's struck me that people are acting weird in Aldamo. Have you noticed?"

"How do you mean 'weird'?"

"It's little things, I guess. Like Tom Foley wasn't washing his car today, and he's never missed a Sunday to wash it."

Corvalis harrumphed. "Not much to go on, Ernie."

"And what about Sam Hodges smoking at the gas station? And that nut who drove off with the gas nozzle still in his gas tank?"

"So people are getting stupider? Is that what you're saying?"

"And Herb. He didn't have to go and blow himself away on account of that fire."

"Losing your job *is* a pretty traumatic experience. This wouldn't be the first time it triggered a suicide."

"Haven't you noticed anything different in Aldamo's citizens?" I asked with a frown of puzzlement.

"I didn't say that."

"Then you agree," I said eagerly.

"I've noticed an increase in stress-related illnesses. That doesn't necessarily mean the town's going crazy, though. I wouldn't go jumping to conclusions."

I shrugged. "Maybe I'm blowing this out of proportion." I looked around the living room. "By the way, where's your wife?"

"Jenny? She's at work."

"On Sunday?"

"You know lawyers. They get paid by the hour."

I felt somewhat relieved having hashed over my misgivings with Corvalis. At least *he* was still normal.

#

As I walked down Corvalis's driveway, the sprinklers in his lawn went on with a whoosh. It struck me as so typically California, with its rain-starved weather, to have the lawn sprinklers turn on every day. Maybe all was as it should be in our tiny town of Aldamo.

But it wasn't, and I knew it.

#

It was sunset. A subtle fog was drifting in from the Pacific Coast, cooling the air. I could smell the scent of the brackish ocean borne in the mist.

I drove past the local strip club *The Filly Mignon* and remarked the all but empty parking lot.

I parked in the lot and went inside.

As I suspected, the joint was deserted.

Nevertheless, a brunette stripper was on stage performing her routine as rock music blared. Aerosmith's "Walk This Way" reverberated throughout the desolate club.

The topless stripper had a lean supple figure. She flirted with a pole onstage.

"There's nobody here," I told her.

"What?" She cupped her ear with her right hand.

"There's nobody here," I said louder.

"I know," she said, continuing to dance.

"Then why are you dancing?"

She yawned. "Because it's my job."

She was dedicated. I would say that for her.

The strip joint was usually jumping at this time of day on the weekend—even if it was Sunday.

"Where is everybody?" I asked.

"It's the economy."

I turned to leave.

"Hey, where you goin'?" she asked. "Don't you want a wink of the pink? Only five more minutes to the moment of truth."

#

I drove to a boulevard stop.

Something was up, I decided. Economy be damned. Aldamo's citizens were breaking their normal routines, and I wanted to know why.

At the intersection, I watched a jeep rear-end an SUV at a neighboring stop sign.

In an access or rage, the SUV driver sped away, screaming out his open window at the top of his lungs, "You fucking bastard!"

The jeep's driver, for his part, flipped the SUV driver the finger.

His face a crimson, twisted mask of rage, the SUV driver, who appeared to be in his forties, executed a U-turn and careered back in the direction of the jeep, whose driver likewise accelerated toward the SUV.

The two cars thundered toward each other and met in an earth-jarring head-on collision. The jeep got the worst of it, but the SUV driver's head broke through his windshield since he wasn't wearing his seatbelt.

His blood-streaked face bled down his throat, which gushed fresh blood as it lay impaled on the shattered, jagged windshield.

"Something's rotten in the state of Denmark," said a homeless black lady, who was shuffling on the side of the road, dressed in rags.

I could not tell if she was talking to me or to herself.

Her hunched body, wearing too many clothes for this mild weather, meandered toward me.

I got out of my car. I could not imagine anyone surviving that horrific accident—or was it an accident at all?

The way I saw it, the two drivers had committed suicide, trying to kill each other and succeeding in their attempts.

The black lady grinned at me with her gap-toothed mouth.

"There's something rotten in the state of Denmark," she repeated.

The jeep caught fire and exploded, deafening me. I winced and started.

"We've got to call the cops," I said.

"The cops are just like them."

I figured her brains were addled from living and sleeping on the streets and eating out of Dumpsters for most of her life. Who wouldn't go nuts leading a life like that?

To humor her I nodded as if I understood her, realizing it was senseless to try to communicate with a derelict that had a few screws loose.

"The whole town's going crazy," she said, as if she could read my mind.

Had she really been noticing the madness of our citizens, as I had? Or was she just a deranged middle-aged bag lady chattering tosh? Skeptical of her acumen, I opted for the latter explanation, which seemed more likely.

"I know," I muttered absently.

Her eyes lit up at my words. "Even the cops."

Was that the wild twinkle of dementia in her brown eyes? I wondered.

"Right," I said.

"You've noticed too?"

"Uh-huh," I said, wondering why I was holding this conversation with a basket case.

"Then we're the only ones along with a couple of others in town who aren't crazy."

I didn't want to spend the rest of the day, what little there was left of it, conversing with a lunatic. I made to leave her.

"Wait," she said. "I can confide in you. You're not one of them."

I waited for her to go on, feeling more like a fool than ever for listening to her bughouse ramblings. "Dr. Morlec's behind all this," she said.

"Who's Dr. Morlec?" I asked.

"He's the new dentist in town. He moved here two weeks ago. He's giving free dental exams to help jump-start his business—at least that's what he says. The town's never been the same since."

"I was out of town for two weeks."

The jeep exploded again, this burst more subdued in its intensity than that of the original blast.

She commenced an Indian chant, dancing and fitfully cupping her open mouth with her hand.

How could I believe anything this loony had to say? I asked myself, watching her wackiness in bafflement.

She ceased her chant. "This isn't the only town that's been infected. It's happening all across the country."

"What is?"

"It's not really an infection, but a rogue cadre of government agents called Section 6 who are taking over the land."

"With dentists?" Incredulous, I suppressed an urge to walk away from her. She had to be bonkers.

"Certain dentists are implanting microchips inside everybody's teeth."

"Why?"

I was only half-listening. Her story was becoming more outlandish by the second. She had missed her true calling in life—she ought to be pitching scripts to Hollywood producers.

She bored her gaze into mine. Her already-swimming eyes seemed to secrete more tears.

"To control people," she said. "The cadre is transmitting signals to the microchips, which in turn stimulate people to work harder and longer."

I raised an eyebrow at that. What she was saying seemed to dovetail with what I had been mulling over myself. Aldamo residents were thinking about only one thing these days—their jobs.

But she was an escapee from bedlam! I told myself. Maybe I was cracking up, too, if I was agreeing with her.

I needed to relax and analyze my thoughts with a cool intellect. Right now a million conflicting ideas were racing through my mind, forestalling me from making any kind of rational decision on what to do next.

"I'm not really crazy," she whispered. "I just want people to think I am, so they won't report me to the authorities."

My skepticism was not tempered.

"I'm part of the resistance," she went on. "We're forming compartmentalized cells across the country to fight the enslavers. I've been assigned to take out Morlec."

"Hold your horses. What's wrong with people wanting to work?"

"Nothing—if that's what they want to do. But Morlec is signaling them to work constantly, so they never get any sleep and they never enjoy themselves. This country was built on the notion that we are entitled to the pursuit of happiness—or did you forget that?"

"You're saying they're being forced to work?"

"Yes. Against their wills." She paused a beat. "And you've seen the results in Aldamo. This 'accident' we just witnessed, for example."

"It was no accident."

"My point, exactly. It was road rage. Deliberate murder by people who are under so much stress from work that they will explode at the slightest provocation."

I weighed what she had said. "Why can't Morlec control the rage? Prevent them from killing each other and themselves?"

"Any kind of violent emotion blocks the transmitting signal from reaching the brain. People revert to their animal instincts and act accordingly."

"Then everybody's going to kill everybody else in town on account of stress? Is that what you're saying?"

"Or they become too tired from overwork and act stupidly, hurting themselves or others."

"Do you really believe this?"

She nodded. "That's what has happened in the other towns."

"How can the Morlecs of the world succeed if everybody's dead?"

"'The amount of work that the slaves produce before they die more than compensates for their disappearance from the work force.' That's a direct quote from Section 6's manual."

"I don't get it."

"Don't you see? When everybody works longer hours, they produce more. When they produce more, profits increase hand over fist. The people on top prosper."

An ambulance siren knifed through the air, followed by the wail of a squad car.

"We better split," she said. "Somebody called the cops."

"Why do we have to split? We didn't do anything wrong."

"I told you, Section 6 owns the cops."

"So?"

' "They don't want witnesses to all these so-called accidents that happen time and time again when Section 6 takes over a town."

Smoke form the jeep drifted in our direction and I started to choke on it. I coughed to clear my burning throat.

"Take care of yourself," she said, and disappeared into the woods.

I didn't know what to make of her as I watched her quirky bulky figure with its awkward gait clash incongruously with the fir trees like a bizarre animal out of its indigenous habitat.

Was she mad or was she using madness as a disguise to mask her knowledge of the truth? I wondered.

In any case, I decided to take her advice and make tracks away from the accident.

Something was definitely wrong in Aldamo, I decided. There was no question of that. Whether Section 6 and Dr. Morlec were behind it I didn't know.

One thing was for sure. I wasn't going to have any of my cavities filled by Morlec. He wasn't the only dentist in town.

All I wanted was the good life. I had no desire to go running around saving the world like James Bond.

But—and this was a big *but*—I could not stand idly by and let everyone in town try to kill each other off, which was exactly what they seemed bound and determined to do. After all, if they continued in this manner unabated, I could well end up one of their victims.

#

I drove toward Tyler Banyon's bungalow.

He was a reporter for Aldamo's local paper *The Clarion*. On account of his job, he knew most everybody in town. Maybe he had the inside skinny on Dr. Morlec.

Dusk was yielding to night, losing its daily battle with the armies of darkness.

Meanwhile, fog was roaming in from the ocean like surreptitious sheep flocking through the trees.

I enjoyed the salty scent of the ocean as I breathed the cool humid air deep into my lungs. For my money, it was the best part of the night or day whenever you could catch the piquant aroma of the nearby sea.

On my way to Banyon's I noticed Harley, the town drunk, picking up aluminum soda cans on the roadside. It was the first time I had ever seen him work at anything.

I slowed my car.

"Are you turning over a new leaf, Harley?" I asked. "Becoming a working man?"

He looked at the plastic bag of soda cans in his hand then up at me.

"I'm not myself lately," he said, and returned to work.

Minutes later, I turned into Banyon's driveway.

He owned a one-story Spanish-styled avocado stucco bungalow, what else?

I knocked on his door.

Banyon answered in his bathrobe, though it could not have been past 7 p.m.

Smoking a stubby cigar he caught me taking in his checkered robe.

"Did I interrupt anything important?" I asked.

"You could say that."

"Should I leave?" I made to go.

"I was trying to get my wife Sherry to give me head."

I chuckled. "Were you getting anywhere?"

"I'll never know now because of you."

"That's right. Blame me for your shortcomings."

"Whoa! That was a low blow and not worthy of you, Ernie. Come in."

I entered his cramped living room.

"I must have the only wife in America who won't give head," he went on.

"I doubt it."

"I can't ask you, because you're not married."

"I wouldn't tell you about it, even if I was."

"She's a liberated woman in every way but that."

"I feel for you, Tyler."

"Oh, can the insincere pity, *puh*-lease."

"I'm surprised you're not working."

Banyon's fortyish, lined face stretched in surprise. "Working? Why on earth would I be working? It's after seven o'clock."

"Everybody else in town is hard at work."

"Not me, Ernie. You know me. I'm a hedonist. I only work because of necessity—and my wife, of course."

"You're the last hedonist in Aldamo."

"I wish I was anywhere else but Aldamo. I belong in the big city with free-thinking broads."

Banyon poured himself a Scotch at the wet bar and sat down.

"Help yourself to a drink," he said.

I grabbed a Corona Light from the miniature refrigerator that sat on the bar. "Don't mind if I do."

"What's this all about? I have a sneaky suspicion this isn't a social call."

"Being a reporter, you know most everyone in town. Right?"

"More or less."

"So what do you know about the new dentist in town—Dr. Morlec?"

He waved me off. "I make a point of never going to the dentist. Life's too short." He smiled.

"I'm serious. Aldamo's going nuts."

"I'm going nuts. Do you think porno videos would help?"

"What are you talking about?"

"Do you think they would help persuade Sherry to give me head?"

"Are you kidding? People are killing themselves, working themselves to death, and that's all you can think about? You're a piece of work, Tyler."

"I never said I was perfect."

"I guess I'm wasting my time here." I set my Corona longneck down on the sideboard.

Banyon cleared his throat. "Did you say people are killing each other?"

"And themselves."

At last, I thought. Banyon's vaunted reporter's instinct was rising to the occasion, however languidly.

I told him about the two drivers who had deliberately crashed into each other, inflamed by road rage. I mentioned Herb's suicide and Sam's death by holocaust, as well.

Banyon's face registered concern. "What's this got to do with Dr. Morlec?"

"Somebody told me he's implanting microchips in his patients' teeth, which send signals to the patients to work themselves to death. You know the old saying—Stress Kills."

Banyon paused. Then he guffawed.

I headed to the front door, irked by his reaction.

"Somebody's pulling your leg," he said.

"I'm telling you, people are cracking up in this berg." I could not hide the ire in my voice.

"Take it easy, Ernie. All I know about Morlec is he's pretty new in town, and he used to work for the government in some capacity."

My ears pricked up when I heard him say *government*.

"Section 6," I muttered.

"I didn't catch that."

I left Banyon there with a confused expression on his furrowed face.

Driving toward my shack I picked up on Harley choking another wino on the roadside. The older wino was clutching an empty soda can to his chest as Harley was trying to pry it away from him with one hand while he choked the geezer with the other.

I honked my horn.

Harley glared at me for interrupting him. His victim managed to break free from Harley's grasp and hobbled away in his filthy rags, still hugging his bent soda can to his chest.

#

I slowed down when I reached my place.

I was naturally suspicious when I saw two prowl cars parked in my dirt driveway.

It looked like they had just arrived. Their light bars were still flashing red and white. The black-and-white cars were empty, so the cops must have been inside my crib.

I didn't like the looks of it. I remembered the bag lady saying Section 6 owned the cops. But why were they looking for me?

Somebody must have ratted me out. But who? And what for?

I had to get out of there but fast. I flashed by my place without even stopping.

#

Sweating at the wheel I desperately needed to confide in someone I could trust. I decided to drive to Jasmine's office.

Jasmine was a part-time optometrist's receptionist, part-time exotic dancer, and, last but not least, my part-time girlfriend.

She liked my paintings. She told me she would become my full-time, full-fledged girlfriend if I ever started selling any of them.

Her office was closed at this hour. She lived out of town.

I yawned, as though all the day's untoward, inexplicable events had suddenly dawned on me and their aggregate exhausted me.

If I didn't catch some shuteye soon, I might start killing people, like everybody else in town seemed bent on doing.

I booked a room in a cheap hotel and was asleep as soon as my head hit the pillow.

#

Early the next morning, I drove to Jasmine's office in a strip mall.

In the parking lot, two women were fighting over a parking space.

A middle-aged woman had parked her ancient gas-guzzling station wagon in the space, while a thirtyish woman fumed inside her politically correct gas-stingy Prius, gesticulating that it was her space.

The woman in the station wagon would not budge.

"I'm late for work!" cried the younger woman in the Prius.

With that she drove her Prius into the station wagon's tailgate and rammed the vehicle out of the parking space.

The middle-aged woman stormed out of her car, screaming, "Bitch!"

The Prius driver's hazel eyes popped out of her head in fury.

She jumped out of her car, withdrew a tire iron from the trunk, stalked toward the other woman, and began clubbing her face with the steel tool.

The middle-aged woman shrieked, clutched her bleeding, shredded face, and collapsed to the asphalt on her knees.

The Prius driver continued wielding her blood-soaked tire iron and smashing the other woman until she fell on her stomach, turned over, and lay supine on the asphalt, her face ruined and bleeding profusely.

Nobody stopped the beating. Everyone was too busy hustling to work, checking their watches, swinging their briefcases, ignoring everything and everybody around them.

I sprinted toward the enraged driver of the Prius and pulled her off the other woman, whose face was beaten to a pulp.

The Prius driver struggled to break free from me at first, but then relaxed, stared at me with mad, sightless hazel eyes, and said, "I'm late for work."

She dropped the blood-splattered tire iron and strode to her company, leaving a trail of blood dripping from her hands.

#

White-faced, shaken, I entered Jasmine's office. I approached her as she sat behind the receptionist's desk.

She acknowledged me. "Shouldn't you be at work, Ernie?"

"I have to talk to you."

"Can't it wait? I'm busy." She shuffled through a congeries of reports that lay on her desktop.

"No, it can't wait!" I exploded. I didn't know how much more of this insanity I could take. I was at my wit's end.

"Shhh! Don't make a scene. Patients are staring at you."

I glared at them as they sat in the waiting room, open magazines on their laps. To hell with them, I decided.

Nevertheless, to please Jasmine, I lowered my voice. "Then I'll talk to you right here," I said.

"I can't talk. I'm too busy."

"You're in the medical profession, Jasmine," I persisted. "Did you ever hear of a Dr. Morlec?"

"Of course."

I waited on tenterhooks for her to elucidate. Maybe I was getting somewhere at last, I thought.

"He's my dentist," she said.

My heart skipped a beat.

What words could describe my horror as I assimilated her words?

She was one of them. Section 6 had gotten to her.

#

I staggered out of her office into the blinding sunlight. It was as though the ground had been pulled out from under me. I stumbled in front of the newspaper vending machine on the sidewalk.

Pablo, my paperboy—more precisely, paper carrier, since he was in his early twenties—was standing there stocking the machine with today's papers.

He was talking to me. I could not make it out. I took in his swarthy bullet head, his black beetled brows.

He was saying in a low voice, "Section 6 is infiltrated by aliens from space." He paused. "We can't talk here. Let's go to my truck."

We walked to his rusty pickup, which was half-full of bound and bundled newspapers.

I wanted to laugh. It wasn't a government conspiracy anymore. Now it was a space-alien conspiracy. Was I losing my mind? I wondered.

I caught sight of Dr. Corvalis hastening past us through the parking lot, his doctor's bag in hand. I was on the verge of hailing him when I noticed the fixed stare of his eyes. He looked intent, oblivious to all around him. I doubted that he saw me. He did not look like the same jovial Dr. Corvalis that I once knew.

I turned away form him, hoping he would not see me. After all, maybe he was the one who had ratted me out to Section 6. He could very well be one of them now. Maybe he had been already, when I last spoke to him.

In any case, I could not trust anyone anymore. I had to go on the assumption that everybody in town had been compromised.

With that in mind, I asked Pablo with distrust, "What's Section 6?"

Puzzlement contorted his face. "Ligeia said she told you about them."

"Ligeia?"

The black lady pretending she's a bag lady."

I kept my face passive, trying to determine whether to trust him or not, whether I should admit that I knew Ligeia.

"I'm part of the resistance," he went on, adjusting the bundles of papers in the back of his truck.

"Whatever," I said, still circumspect.

"Section 6 is an elite government counterterrorist organization, like Ligeia told you. What she didn't tell you is that Section 6 is being run by aliens from space. Their intent is clear."

"Not to me."

"They're paving the way for colonization of the earth."

I could not believe my ears. "By becoming dentists?" I said, sarcasm dripping from my lips.

"They have the ability to assume human form. They're parasites. They feed off humans while they infest them."

"They look like us. Is that what you're saying?"

"Exactly. They're spitting images of us. They walk like us. They talk like us. But they're not us. They're bent on enslaving and destroying us in the process."

"This is preposterous!"

"I didn't say it was believable. But it's true."

I took this in with a grain of salt. "What's with all this *work, work, work* they keep yakking about?"

Pablo nodded, as if expecting the question. "They're working us to death for two reasons. First, to get as much production out of us as possible, so that they themselves won't have to work. And, second, to kill us by making us kill each other or ourselves because of burn-out."

"How do they infest our bodies?"

"Certain dentists are impregnating our bodies with them."

"Morlec?"

"Yes. The aliens enter our bodies through the nerves in our teeth."

"I never go to the dentist."

"That's why you're still free, and why we need you in the resistance. The aliens are everywhere. They could be your next-door neighbors."

Tom Foley? I wondered.

Out of the corner of my eye, I picked up on Dr. Corvalis again. He was hustling toward his Mercedes.

I held my hand to my face so he would not recognize me.

"We have to get out of here," I told Pablo.

"I know. Especially you. You're on their hit list. They suspect you know about them, so they're going to drill your teeth and occupy your body."

"I'm going to see Morlec."

"Are you crazy? He'll turn you into one of them in his dentist's chair."

Pablo grabbed my shoulders and shook them as if trying to shake sense into me.

"I gotta see if any of what you say about him is true," I said. "It's just too damn far-fetched."

Warily, I watched him pull a handgun out of the back of his truck. I tensed. When he pressed it into my right hand, I relaxed.

"At least, take this," he urged, squeezing my hand for a second.

"All right." I didn't need to be told twice. "And I'm going in disguise."

"I'll go with you as backup."

#

The last thing I wanted to do was go to the dentist.

I had to get to the bottom of this, though.

Pablo drove me to a mom-and-pop costume store at a minimall. Inside the store, I bought cheap sunglasses, an Angels baseball cap, and a wig.

He drove me to Morlec's office complex. I didn't notice anybody tailing us. That was a load off my mind.

"I'll wait here for you," said Pablo, as he parked his pickup in the lot in front of the three-story office building.

Wearing my disguise I walked into the office complex, trying to alter my natural gait by adding a roll favoring my right. I hunched my right shoulder to contribute to the effect.

Palms sweaty, my heart pounding in my ears, I entered Morlec's office.

"Hello," said the middle-aged secretary, her grizzled hair pulled up in a tight bun. "Do you have an appointment with the doctor?"

"No," I said, and cupped my right cheek with my hand. "This is an emergency. My tooth is killing me."

"You need an appointment."

"I feel like I'm dying," I groaned.

The secretary frowned. "Wait a second. I'll have to check with the doctor." She left her cubicle.

I ducked out of the waiting room into the corridor and followed her, unbeknownst to her.

She led me to Morlec. In the dental chair beside him was a patient who was prepped to have her teeth drilled. Morlec was examining his drill.

The secretary spoke to Morlec out of earshot. I saw him nod. She turned around in my direction.

I bolted into a vacant office behind me. After she passed by, I approached Morlec's office and watched him from behind a column in the hallway.

He looked like any other doctor, or teacher, for that matter, with his bushy white hair and thick-framed black plastic glasses.

Could this innocuous-looking guy possibly be a space alien hatching plots for world conquest? I wondered.

It seemed unlikely. And yet . . . something was happening in Aldamo, something that was transforming its laid-back denizens into homicidal maniacs.

I watched Morlec and waited.

He inserted a drill into his patient's propped-open mouth. He drilled a tooth for a few minutes. Then he swung the drill aside and opened his mouth.

I stood transfixed as I watched his tongue slither past his blubbery purple, saliva-coated lips.

Slither was the only word I could think of, because it was like no human tongue I had ever seen. In fact, it was metallic silver and looked more like a snake than like a tongue.

Indeed, it sank into his patient's gaping mouth and burrowed its way into the hole that Morlec had drilled into her tooth.

She screamed in agony as Morlec's tongue probed deeper and deeper into her nervous system, into her entire body, it seemed—because there was no end to the tongue.

It was infesting every nerve in her body, feeding off her nervous system, occupying her. Enslaving her.

Morlec's eyes turned fluorescent green, bathing his office in a sickly pea-soup-colored glow.

I had seen enough.

I had to get out of there on the double.

In my haste, I knocked over a water cooler in the corridor. The ensuing crash attracted Morlec's attention.

I slipped on the water that was pouring all over the linoleum floor and fell on my back.

The thing that was Morlec walked toward me, its obscene tongue now dripping with his patient's blood, dangling eight feet out of his foaming mouth, slithering like a sidewinder across the floor as if it had a life of its own, hissing with anticipation ahead of Morlec in its eagerness to reach me.

It was too much.

My stomach turned. I struggled to free the revolver from my waistband. On my back, I trained the Smith & Wesson's barrel on Morlec's head and fired. My first two bullets missed their mark.

The third one struck Morlec spang in the face and stopped him in his tracks.

His tongue kept winding toward me, however.

I emptied my gun at it, but it was impossible to hit for its thinness and its constant whipping motion.

I sprang to my feet.

The tongue was moving slower toward me now as it approached the water on the floor. Was it apprehensive of the water? I wondered.

I kicked water on it. Sparks jumped from it as it squealed like a stuck pig and jerked away.

I flew out of there like I was shot out of a cannon.

"Resistance is futile!" cried the secretary when she saw me bucket by her.

#

I jumped into the passenger seat of Pablo's pickup.

He screeched its smoking wheels as he put on speed.

His eyes bulging, he asked, "Will you join the resistance? There are Morlecs all over the country."

I nodded, catching my breath.

"We can't let them take over," I gasped.

"We've got to warn people."

"Let's call the FBI." Worked up, I shook my fist.

Pablo shot me a consternated glance. "They could be infiltrated by a fifth column of aliens."

I paused, my fist still clenched. "Then we're on our own."

And I knew what that was like.

Yeah. I knew what that was like.

Feast of Bones

There was something about her eyes . . .

Carston Lennox III had learned from his hero, the serial killer Jeffrey Dahmer, that it took an hour to boil a human head before you could eat it. This Lennox had never dreamed of doing before.

Being a senator from California, he had no trouble picking up beautiful women. They were a dime a dozen, in fact. They were charmed by his charismatic smile, the same easy smile that had won him elections. The difficulty, and what gave excitement to his life, lay in hiding his assignations from the prying eyes of the omnipresent press.

He was running for reelection this year and to this day he had never boiled a girl's head, had never even thought of it, till he had read in the papers about Jeffrey Dahmer, the Milwaukee Cannibal, doing it.

Lennox did indeed collect body parts, because the reason that he killed these women was to make them stay with him. He could not marry them for he was already married. The only way he could possess them forever, which was the reason he wanted them, was to do them and keep their bodies.

I now pronounce you man and wife, he thought with a wry smile.

Keeping their entire corpses would have been impossible on account of their very size. In lieu of that he would hack mementoes off their cadavers, such as, fingers, toes, ears, noses, nipples, etc.—you get the idea—and take them home with him. (He even made a necklace out of two ears that he had appropriated from a brunette with the help of a cutthroat razor.) Then he would store the mementoes inside his freezer at his mansion in Sacramento.

To do all this under the glare of the media spotlight and get away with it was a thrill beyond belief, decided Lennox. Maybe he should run for president. The glare would be twice as harsh then. That would ramp up the thrill factor tenfold.

Was he insane? he wondered. But if he was, how could he have been elected senator of California? Could a madman possibly be elected to public office? Wouldn't the populace see through his veneer of sanity?

Lennox decided it was the power of his personality and of his charisma that attracted votes and beautiful women. Power exuded from his every pore and he needed to possess women to satisfy his cravings for more power. Women sensed the overwhelming musk he emitted and succumbed to him willy-nilly—gladly, for that matter.

The possessing of another human being was the most powerful thing a man could do, decided Lennox. All men thrived on power. Nietzsche explained it as the *will to power.* And he, Lennox, as a politician, was the highest form of man, evolving into the *Ubermensch*, or superman.

#

The only power LA police detective Irene Maxwell knew was the power that emanated from the barrel of a gun. She liked playing the piano for Sami at night and firing her 9 mm Browning automatic at a shooting range in the morning. In her forties, she liked to believe music kept her sane in a world that stood but one remove from chaos.

She was always on the lookout for chaos— the murderer in his home, the thief casing a bank, the rapist staking out nightclubs in back alleys. Wherever the purveyors of chaos might be, Maxwell would be there, too, waiting for them to tip their hands. She liked to think that, anyway . . .

"A penny for them," said Haggerty, the middle-aged stocky detective with a butch haircut who was sitting beside her.

"I can smell him," said Maxwell.

"Smell who?" Haggerty bowed his chubby face and made a show of sniffing his armpits.

"Knock it off, Jack," she said with a fleeting smile playing across her lips. "You know who."

"You know what your problem is?"

"Yeah. You."

"No. You're alone too much. You start talking weird when you're alone all the time."

Maxwell didn't say anything for a while. She was annoyed at Haggerty for broaching the subject. She wanted to let it slide.

Then: "I'm not alone," she said. "I have Sami."

"Sami's a fucking parrot, Irene."

"Sami's good company." She paused a beat. "Not like you."

Haggerty shook his head, one edge of his mouth turned down. "OK, I'll play along. So who do you smell, Irene?"

"The serial killer."

"That's rich," Haggerty scoffed. "What's he wearing? Lemme guess. Brut aftershave?"

She turned away from her driving and gave him a look.

"C'mon, Irene," he said.

She faced the road in front of her, guiding the steering wheel with her hands at three o'clock and nine o'clock. "He's around, I tell you. He's around."

"How do you know?"

"I don't know it. I feel it."

"*Aye-yi-yi!* So now you got ESP. Gimme a break."

She ignored his sarcasm and muttered, "He's around."

"You're the one who's around. Around the bend." Haggerty laughed at his joke.

"At least, now we have a suspect."

Haggerty harrumphed. "Do you have any idea what a can of worms we're gonna open when we interrogate this guy? When the media sharks hear about this . . . You know they can smell blood for miles."

"Are you finished?"

#

Lennox was walking through the hall on the

top floor of the massive, white-painted Beverly Hilton Hotel, heading for an assignation with a drop-dead brunette heiress with sloe eyes. This was the first time he had encountered a woman with sloe eyes, he mused, though he had read about them in books.

Beside him was his spin doctor, Tom Hawes. They had just finished attending a fund-raiser in the ballroom and Hawes was talking to him about which part of his speech to use in a sound bite for the air waves.

"I'll leave the decision up to you," Lennox told him, trying to get rid of him.

Nobody in Lennox's entourage, not even Tom, his closest advisor, had the faintest inklings about his assignations. And Tom, Lennox knew for sure, did not know about Lennox's date tonight with the luscious Beverly Hills heiress Sandra, the daughter of a filthy rich movie mogul.

There was something about Denise's blue eyes . . .

Lennox's heart was beating faster. Adrenaline was jacking him up. Somehow, he was thinking, he had to ditch Tom. The guy was still walking with him down the plush oxblood-carpeted corridor, mumbling gibberish about sound bites. As if Lennox gave a damn.

"Immigration's a hot-button issue," Tom was saying. "Your opponent wants to keep all the illegals out of the country."

"Yeah," said Lennox, not listening, his mind elsewhere, thinking of what Sandra looked like buck naked.

To get her hot Lennox was going to show

her one of his porno DVDs that he toted around with him in his luggage. Every hotel he had ever lodged at had a DVD player hooked up to its color TV nowadays. Either that or X-rated movies available on their pay TV stations. It was only a matter of time before they all had high-definition TVs as well.

"The Japs make all the DVD players," Lennox said absently.

"What's that got to do with immigration, Cars? And don't say 'Japs,' for Chrissake. It's politically incorrect. Say 'Japanese.'"

To a man Lennox's friends called him Cars, short for Carston Lennox III. The son of a Wisconsin brewery magnate, he had graduated from Yale, summa cum laude, a Skull and Bones man.

Yes, thought Lennox, a handful of Yale students had always been recruited by secret organizations patterned after the Mafia, like the Skull and Bones Club. You could not apply to these organizations, Lennox knew. Either they recruited you or they didn't, period.

Lennox decided his charming smile must have intrigued them, plus, of course, his father's millions.

In Skull and Bones, Lennox made essential connections with well-fixed blue bloods, who would later pave his way into politics. Without their help he never would have become a success story as a senator.

"We'll let our illustrious opponent hang himself on the immigration issue—" said Tom.

"What?"

"Look. He'll sound like a racist, like he

hates the Mexicans who cross the border illegally. We'll stand by and let him hoist himself on his own petard."

Was he still jabbering away? wondered Lennox, eager to part company with him. Lennox was pumped up and wanted to have at Sandra. He wanted to fuck her brains out and saw her head off.

He wanted to see if what Dahmer had said was true—that it took an hour to boil a human head. In any case, it was going to be a bloody mess, Lennox could see. What would happen if he sawed her head off in the bathtub? Lennox wondered. There the blood would drain out, leaving nothing for him to clean up. Lennox congratulated himself on his cleverness.

"I have a headache, Tom. I want to be alone in my suite."

There was something about Denise's eyes, the way they looked at me . . .

"OK," said Tom. "It's been a long day." His boyish, bespectacled face looked drawn as if to confirm his words. "Good night."

Tom took leave of Lennox.

To his shock Lennox picked up a security guard patrolling the hallway.

"Tom," said Lennox, as Tom was peeling off. "Why is that security guard here?"

"Don't you remember?"

"No." Lennox shook his head in confusion.

"You got a death threat over the phone this morning."

"So what else is new? Business as usual. What's the big deal?"

"Just a precaution. The guard, I mean."

"Tell him to get lost. He reminds me of a turnkey."

Tom shrugged as if it did not matter to him one way or the other. "No problem."

He talked to the beefy rent-a-cop and they shoved off together.

When Lennox opened the door to his suite, using the magnetic card key, he was surprised to find Sandra already inside, wearing a clingy flamingo pink minidress. Had the rent-a-cop seen her enter his suite? Lennox wondered, or had she arrived before he had taken up position outside Lennox's door?

She smiled at the surprise that registered on his face, which surfaced despite his adept skills at dissimulation, which was second nature to pols, Lennox knew.

"How many women have you screwed, Senator Lennox?" she asked, leaning backwards, sizing him up, a drink in her hand.

She had found the cellarette, Lennox realized, and had helped herself to a bottle of J&B Scotch that now stood open on top of the cellarette. She could not have been more than twenty-five, decided Lennox, but she acted like the queen of England.

She angled toward Lennox with an unsteady gait. For that matter, she looked drunk.

"As many as JFK?" she said in response to her own question as Lennox stood nonplussed by her presence.

At length he pulled himself together and asked, "How did you get in here?"

"I used a master card key. My daddy is part

owner of this hotel."

"Did the rent-a-cop see you come in?"

"What rent-a-cop?"

He must not have been in the hall when she arrived, Lennox surmised. He sighed with relief but let nothing show on his face. By now he had returned to being the consummate politician.

She came closer, drawn by his charisma.

He glanced at her décolletage and smelled death. It was a sweet cloying odor–somewhat like a ripe fart. He was no stranger to the stench. It aggravated him, jump-started his heart. She reeked of booze and death.

"How many women have you laid?" she demanded, her tone all but hostile.

He sidled toward the closet, in which he had secreted his hacksaw. It would be strong enough to sever her throat. He had used it on enough fingers and toes to know it could even sever bone.

The way Denise's eyes looked when I killed her. They looked . . .

"How many women have you knocked off?" she insisted.

Lennox's heart stopped and a frisson went down his spine. Could she possibly know of the other women he had done away with? he wondered. Then he remembered that *knocked off* was a euphemism for *screwing* as well as for *killing*. Wasn't it?

"Aren't you man enough for me?" she goaded.

She set down her drink on the cellarette and shucked off her stretch minidress over her head like it was a long T-shirt. She stood in her bloodred panties and demibra. Her neck set to swaying from side to side, her eyes closed, and she snapped her fingers as if listening to imaginary rock music. She was humming a tune that he could not identify.

He decided he wanted to murder her with his hands, not with the hacksaw. She was drunk enough so that he would not have to spike her drink with Halcion to prevent her from putting up resistance.

Very often he used his hands to kill. For one thing it was cleaner. No blood to mop up. It was simply a matter of placing his arm around her neck, pressing her vagus nerve against his wrist, and destroying it with a quick snap.

Death was instantaneous, as any good hangman knew, reflected Lennox. Only a piker of a hangman killed by strangling his victim, and that could take hours with the victim kicking and foaming at the mouth and sticking his tongue out and bugging out his eyes and gnashing his teeth and defecating. *Jesus!* thought Lennox, it sounded like fun. The problem was, Lennox knew, the victim might live and rat you out.

But there was something about Denise's eyes . . .

He repaired to the kitchen.

"Where are you going?" asked Sandy.

"To get an olive for my drink."

"I can't wait," she said huskily.

He opened the brushed aluminum refrigerator door, reached back behind the cartons of low-fat milk, and withdrew a tall narrow olive jar.

He held the jar up to the light and looked

through the clear glass at the orbs that floated in the formaldehyde, at the eyes of some of his victims, at Denise's blue eyes, which bobbed up and down against each other, the topmost eyes—because he had to know what there was about them that kept sticking in his mind.

"What's taking you so long?" cried Sandy, and he heard her footfalls approaching.

Like a shot he replaced the olive jar in the refrigerator and shut its door.

The way Denise's eyes looked . . . but I still don't get it! . . .

He returned to Sandy in the living room.

The creamy swell of her breasts in her bra excited him. They reeked of booze and death and intoxicated his brain. Her fat nipples sprouted up like stalks of corn and pressed through her sheer bra, jutting up, attracted to the sun of his face.

His mind was reeling on account of the heady perfume of death and aroused-breast smell, but he knew he could not haul her ashes until after he had whacked her out to prevent her from being able to take a powder after they partied. That was the thing—if you partied with a stiff, Lennox knew, it could never leave you and would be yours forever.

He flashed his telegenic smile at her and she was ready to melt in his arms. The telltale moisture on her panties made no bones about the stimulated condition of her experienced pudenda.

His mind was evanescing into rufous mist. It was difficult for him to put a lid on the urge that was overcoming him at the sight of her half-naked figure. Seeing her arousal he realized he would not have to show her a porn flick to turn her on.

He worked his way around her as she slid out of her panties with a slinky gyrating of her rounded hips and springy can, anticipating his urge to take her from behind. Before she had a chance to bend forward and offer her bottom to him he hooked his left arm around her neck, wedged her throat in the crook of his arm, and applied a choke hold with leverage from his right arm.

"Hold me," she said, and he snapped her vagus nerve. That killed her. She sort of cried out like a mewing kitty when she died.

As luck would have it, she did not void her bowels, so he would not have to swab up the mess. Sometimes his victims defecated on dying, but it was more or less a fifty-fifty proposition, he knew. Thank goodness this was a clean kill!

He dragged her toward the bathroom, and his heart came to a complete halt as somebody knocked on the front door. *Jesus Christ!* Lennox thought. Who the hell could that be? he wondered. He wasn't expecting visitors.

Still bent over the cadaver, he called, "Who is it?" through the suite's door.

"LAPD."

Oh sure, he thought. They just happened to be outside his door when he whacked out Sandy. Then he thought, his mind working furiously, recalling what Tom had told him earlier, maybe they wanted to talk to him about the death threat he had got in the morning. Yes, Lennox decided, that must be it. Bad timing, to say the least.

"One minute," he said and hauled Sandy into the bathroom.

Her naked body squeaked across the smooth linoleum like rubber soles. Lennox hoped the cops could not hear the deafening ruckus.

Grunting with the effort of hefting her dead weight he dumped her in the bathtub and slid the pebbled-glass gold-framed shower door shut. He left the bathroom door ajar so the cops would not see it shut and think somebody was inside. He flung her discarded clothes under the sofa cushions in the living room.

Then he took three deep breaths to compose himself, combed his hair, smoothed his thousand-dollar Armani jacket with his hands, opened the door to the suite, and asked, "Can't this wait?" in an unruffled voice.

"'Fraid not, Senator," said Maxwell. "It's sort of an emergency. About a murder investigation."

"It can't wait?" said Lennox, puzzlement on his face, which wore exactly the cast he wanted on it.

"I'm Detective Maxwell, homicide. This is Detective Haggerty behind me." She motioned with her head toward Haggerty.

Haggerty, Lennox noted, was a middle-aged guy with a butch haircut (a coiffure that Lennox detested). Haggerty smiled at Lennox over Maxwell's shoulder.

Haggerty had a suety complexion that afforded his face an unctuous expression when he smiled. He would have made a great priest, Lennox decided, except for the earthworm-thick pulsing purple vein that bulged out of his forehead, which might scare away prospective parishioners.

Whatever he thought of Haggerty, Lennox did not let on and smiled back at him.

"Could we come in?" asked Maxwell, the picture of politeness.

Maxwell wasn't a bad-looking woman, decided Lennox, but she didn't do anything for him. Truth to tell, she turned him off. She had an air about her, a certain sanctimoniousness, that he found offensive in the extreme.

It would have looked suspicious if Lennox had said no to her request, so he said yes, and the two cops strode in.

Haggerty stepped up to Lennox and, smiling, held out his hand for Lennox to shake, which Lennox did, though he thought it presumptuous of Haggerty. Lennox figured that by being polite he could get shut of them faster, without arousing their suspicions.

"I voted for ya, Senator. Glad ta meet ya," said Haggerty.

"Likewise. What can I do for you?"

"Didja know Denise Kupek?" asked Haggerty.

Lennox twigged that Haggerty was looking around the suite and taking in the bathroom, so he answered in jig time to preoccupy Haggerty's attention.

"No," Lennox said.

"That's funny."

"How so?"

Haggerty stroked his coffee-colored dense mustache with a finger and thumb. "'Cause her sister says Denise went out with you one night." Haggerty bored his beady blue eyes into Lennox's wide-spaced green ones.

Lennox did not like Haggerty's insinuating and accusative attitude one bit. Being wealthy Lennox was used to having people fawn all over him, not to having them confront him like this lowlife standing in front of him was doing.

Haggerty smiled and winked at him then leaned toward Lennox confidentially. "Like 'em young, huh, Senator. That's no crime. We all like a good-lookin' piece a tail."

Maxwell rolled her eyes but did not say anything.

Lennox cringed at Haggerty's suffocating propinquity. He felt himself commencing to despise the genial Haggerty. This ragtag and bobtail, Lennox decided, had the audacity to pretend that he was Lennox's equal and his friend to boot.

"Don't let Haggerty get under your skin," said Maxwell. She glanced at Haggerty then went on to Lennox, "He has a way of doing that."

"Just answer the question, Senator," said Haggerty, trying to ignore Maxwell's dig.

"I don't remember her," Lennox lied.

Maxwell said, "A driver of an eighteen-wheeler found her naked corpse dumped on the shoulder of the San Diego Freeway near Sherman Oaks. She had a broken neck."

"She was raped and sodomized after she died," chipped in Haggerty.

The loathsome Haggerty, editorialized Lennox to himself, but said, "How awful."

"Her left pinky was missing," said Maxwell.

I don't have it, Lennox was tempted to say

but thought better of it. After all, they had not accused him of having it, so why should he deny it? Instead of speaking, he shook his head in commiseration.

"Her eyes were missing too," said Maxwell, searching Lennox's face.

"That's . . ."

Lennox did not know what to say. *Her eyes . . . they looked familiar somehow.*

"Are you sure you don't remember her?" Maxwell asked Lennox, sounding as though she found it hard to believe.

"I meet a lot of people in my profession, Detective. I can't remember everybody. Maybe I shook her hand in a crowd. I don't know."

"Surely if you had a date with her you would remember her."

"Especially since it was only a week ago," said Haggerty, again flashing his greasy smile at Lennox.

Lennox smiled back at him just as smoothly, looking calm and cool. "I don't recall it." This was as easy as running for election, decided Lennox: *keep lying with a smiling face and everyone will believe you, no matter how egregious the lie.*

"She had red hair and blue eyes and a spray of freckles on her face," said Maxwell. She touched her cheeks to indicate the whereabouts of Denise's freckles.

"I don't recall her."

"Well, this gets even weirder. This story her sister tells us. She says Denise was her adopted sister. She says Denise said you were her real father."

"According to her sister, Denise claimed you abandoned her when she was a child," added Haggerty.

"Forgive us for asking, Senator," said Maxwell, "but is there any truth to what Denise told her sister?"

"Senator?" said Haggerty.

"Why would she want to date her own father?" Lennox managed to say through a tight throat.

"It was a pretext, Denise's sister told us. Denise knew you have the hots for the girlies and this was the only way she figured she could ever meet you."

"You never returned any of her calls or answered her letters," said Maxwell. "It's a sad story, really."

"I don't have a daughter named Denise," Lennox said. He was losing control of his voice.

"Maybe the parents who brought her up gave her that name. Maybe her birth parents gave her a different name."

"Are you all right, Senator?" said Haggerty. "You look sick."

Lennox's knees did indeed feel weak and his face must have appeared pale. He could feel the blood draining from it.

"Something I ate," he said. "I need some air."

Lennox made for the window, and, seeing the reflection of his eyes in the glass, with a chill running up his spine, realized why Denise's eyes looked familiar.

Her voice rising, Maxwell said, "Senator,

watch your step near that window—"
    "Senator!"

Torment

"What is the name of this organization?" asked Boss Frank.

"There is no love here," the workers answered in unison.

"I thought it was 'Divide and Conquer,'" Marvin wisecracked sotto voce to Jack.

Jack smirked despite himself. *What a place to work*, he thought. He found himself wondering for the umpteenth time why didn't he just quit?

The sixtyish Marvin, who had twenty-odd years on Jack, ran his fingers ever so gently through his sparse white hair that was turning yellow. If Marvin was gentle enough, maybe his tallowy white hair might not fall out, decided Jack.

Jack glanced at Marvin, who rolled his eyes.

Standing in front of them and the other workers, a conveyor belt behind him, Boss Frank blew his nose. Blood spewed out on his handkerchief. He balled up the mess.

"With that in mind, let's kick ass, you bums!" he went on. "That's why my father named this organization 'Smash.' Because *smashing* the competition is what we're all about!"

Nobody cheered. You could have heard a pin drop, decided Jack.

Most of the workers looked sick. Others exchanged hostile glances.

"He loves to make us feel like dirt," muttered Marvin.

On account of the funereal silence, unfortunately for Marvin, Boss Frank overheard the remark.

"What did I just say, Marvin?"

"You said we smash—" Marvin started nervously.

"I said, there is no love here," Boss Frank cut in.

Actually, it was the workers who had said that, Jack wanted to correct him, but didn't.

Marvin nodded. His hunched shoulders tensed.

"I don't love making you feel anything," said Boss Frank. "How do you feel about retirement, Marvin? You look old enough to use a bedpan and walker."

Several of Boss Frank's toadies sniggered.

"Or how about termination, Marvin? You're not exactly our most productive worker."

Boss Frank blew another splotch of crimson blood into his hanky.

Sartre was right, decided Jack. Hell *was* other people.

"Anybody got a problem with our motto?" asked Boss Frank. He glowered at the workers. "Good. Remember it and let's kick the competition's collective ass!"

He stuck his pinky in his right ear and twisted it inside. Blood trickled out of his ear canal and down his neck. He towered before them, all six-feet-five of him, waiting for any sign of resistance. He hawked phlegm and spat it out on the floor.

"Clean it up," he said.

Marvin hustled forward, knelt down, and started to wipe the mucus up with his handkerchief.

"Not that way," said Boss Frank. "With your tongue."

Marvin made a face. He looked back at Jack and implored him to help him with morose, watery green eyes.

Jack did not respond.

Humiliated, Marvin licked the mucus off the floor.

"Guess you don't want to get terminated, huh, geezer?" crowed Boss Frank.

He left the room, laughing to himself, his bulk shaking with merriment in his three-piece grey suit.

On the floor, Marvin looked sick with frustration, embarrassment, and repressed anger, and underneath all of them, as far as Jack could see, an icy sheet of fear. Disgusted with himself and with what little there was of Boss Frank's mucus in his handkerchief, Marvin jammed it into his rear trouser pocket.

Jack could hear Boss Frank singing in the background:

"Oh mares eat oats,
And does eat oats,
And little lambs eat ivy.

A kid'll eat ivy too.
Wouldn't you?"

Afraid of being seen with Marvin, everybody backed away from him.

Marvin had trouble getting to his feet. Jack wanted to help him, but he did not want to lose his job. After all, decided Jack, Boss Frank might see him give Marvin a hand.

Jack retreated to his station and counted the parcels on a nearby pallet.

Marvin groaned as he struggled to stand, then returned to work, looking sheepish.

What was happening to him? Jack wondered. He was too scared, too damn buffaloed to help a harmless old man to his feet. Jack had to get out of this place. There had to be a better way to make a living. Or, and this thought made his skin crawl, was he too far under Boss Frank's thumb to quit and find another job?

Was there really any way out of this job from hell?

Middle-aged Joe Buck, a company clerk, sidled up to Jack and asked, "Are you in on the football pool?"

"Not yet."

"It's ten bucks."

"I wanna see the Vegas line before I put down any money."

"Friday's the deadline."

Joe Buck started to walk away, dragging his club foot. He stopped, leaned toward Jack, and whispered, "Boss Frank's wired the bathroom with parabolic mikes and fiber-optic video cameras."

Jack wished he was surprised by Buck's revelation, but in truth he had expected it—if not now, then in the near future.

"It was only a matter of time," he said.

"We can't even take a leak in private anymore."

"What does he think's going on in there?"

"Who knows? He's a paranoid schizo." Joe unwrapped a stick of Juicy Fruit gum and slipped it into his mouth. He sighed. "Back to work." Then he snarled, "Fucking life, fucking world, fucking job."

"How can you stand working for this guy?"

"How can *you*?"

"Something called food and shelter."

"Another day in paradise." Joe pointed his forefinger at Jack and winked.

"It doesn't get any better than this."

Even the building depressed Jack—what with its institutional green walls, wire mesh glass windows that would not open, and fluorescent strip lights that provided scant light. It had all the makings of a prison.

Boss Frank swaggered down the aisle toward them. His pasty amorphous face floated closer, a trickle of blood beneath his left nostril.

"What's this all about?" he barked.

"I just said hello to Jack," said Joe.

"Yeah. And nobody's got an angle," jeered Boss Frank.

Jack remained silent.

"Break it up and get back to work. The only thing your hides are good for is lamp shades."

Boss Frank decamped. As he approached his office, a rat scurried out in front of him. Without breaking stride, he crushed it to death under his heel. Its squeal died with it.

"That guy gets weirder and weirder," Joe muttered to Jack.

"Didn't he ever hear of an exterminator?"

"He looks like he enjoys doing it himself."

"Marvin!" cried Boss Frank, eying the crushed rat on the floor. "Got another job for your tongue." He chortled.

"That fuck," whispered Joe.

#

Jack drove his tan delivery truck down Wilshire Boulevard to Santa Monica. He turned right on Euclid and parked in front of a pink adobe apartment house.

He could not wait to get away form Boss Frank and the Smash Corporation. Even hauling heavy parcels around all day beat being cooped up inside that dismal Smash warehouse.

On the apartment house's frontage a single palm tree arched thirty feet into the clear blue December sky.

He had a parcel to deliver to Melody. He was eager to see her. Usually she was working in the garden when he delivered to her. He did not see her at the moment. He withdrew her parcel from the back of the truck and made for the apartment house's entrance. He spotted her in the foyer.

She was carrying a green gardening trowel. She was also wearing one of her low-cut, sheer, bra-optional minidresses that exposed an eyeful of cleavage and white thigh.

She must have been wearing a bra today, Jack decided, because her breasts were squeezed together for an effect of maximum fullness. Two beautiful scoops of vanilla ice cream. She was probably wearing one of those Wonder bras—as if she needed one.

He had been working up the courage to ask her out on a date for weeks now.

"Hello, Melody," he said.

"Oh, hello." She smiled at him. Her blue eyes twinkled. She always smiled at him, which led him to believe she was interested in pursuing a relationship.

Any other day he would have chatted her up, but today he dispensed with the small talk and cut to the chase.

"Wanna go on a date Saturday night?" he managed to ask through a tight throat. He was confident that no matter however apprehensive he might have felt, he sounded cool.

She looked more or less embarrassed and shifted awkwardly in her daisy-printed dress, her shoulders stooping and her long legs looking somehow gangly now, as if they weren't part of her, as if she wanted to disown the enticing pair.

"I can't, Jack. I'm married. He won't let me."

He should have known. On the other hand, her packages never said *Mrs.* on them, not that wives used *Mrs.* nowadays. The good ones were always married, he decided in dismay.

"Leave my package now. Thank you, sir," she said, sounding annoyed and superior, wanting to put as much distance between them as possible by adding *sir* to her request.

He laid the package on the ecru linoleum tiles at her feet, nonplussed.

"Goodbye, sir," she announced, encouraging him to leave on the double.

He could not move. It had taken him weeks to screw himself up to ask her out and now it was over just like that—all for nought. He was standing there feeling like an idiot, egg on his face, his ears red—like a teenager who had just been rejected.

It wasn't as if she was the first girl he had ever asked out. What was happening to him? Why was he acting like—*like such a wimp*?

Her rejection of him was a vicious blow to his self-esteem, which was already in tatters, courtesy of Boss Frank. The guy was gelding him in all aspects of his life—the personal as well as the professional side.

How could he have been so wrong about her? Jack wondered. Surely she had been flirting with him from day one—smiling at him, bending over in front of him, showing more and more cleavage . . . But that was all it was—flirting.

What made him think that married women stopped flirting once they got married? She had been raising her self-esteem by making herself desirable to him—but that was as far as it went.

He got the feeling that she had played him for a sap, made use of him to increase her vanity, casting him off like so much slag when he put the moves on her.

There was no question about it: he felt like a king-size jerk.

He sat in his truck and watched her dig in her garden. He felt walled in by unbreakable glass, and no matter how hard he fought he could not free himself from this living tomb.

She noticed him watching her and gave him a long look.

He didn't want her to get angry at him. He wanted to get out of there. He split.

#

The next day he delivered a manila envelop to her. He noticed that it was from a law firm.

She wasn't home. He felt relieved. He had no desire to see her after yesterday. As she had instructed him on earlier occasions, he left the envelope at her doorstep.

He returned to his truck in a brown study. Could the envelope have anything to do with his asking her out? he wondered.

What if she was going to file sexual harassment charges against him and sue Smash? That would drive Boss Frank up the wall. He would can Jack in the blink of an eye rather than face a lawsuit.

Had she set him up? Jack wondered. Had her flirtation been an act so she could sue Smash for millions? He found that hard to believe. But, after all, it was a litigious society and everybody was out to make a fast buck come hell or high water.

He wanted to talk this problem over with somebody, but he could not—*dared not*—tell anyone at the company, for the place was swimming with sharks and backstabbers who would do anything to get ahead, including ratting out a fellow employee.

Maybe he was being too negative about this whole deal. He decided to reexamine the situation. What were Melody's exact words when he asked her out?

"I can't, Jack. I'm married. He won't let me."

Yeah, that was it, Jack decided. Her words were engraved on his mind like pain. *He won't let me.* She was blaming her husband for preventing her from dating Jack. Maybe Jack had overreacted to her rejection.

Maybe, but this seemed to be stretching it, maybe she wanted to hire a lawyer so that she could divorce her husband and go out with Jack. Hence the letter from the lawyer. No. Jack wasn't that full of himself. He could not buy into that interpretation.

Perhaps, the lawyer had nothing to do with him and Melody, Jack decided. She may have needed legal representation for another matter altogether.

Yet, Smash had deep pockets, and sexual harassment lawsuits were the going rage these days.

Any way you cut it, Jack had problems. He had to stay away from Melody and hope she would not report him to Boss Frank. Jack did not know what to do.

#

That night he drove his car to Melody's apartment. He parked across the street from it and watched it. He didn't see her the whole time. He could not shake the feeling that he was entombed in glass.

All he did was ask her out on a date for Chrissake! Was that against the law these days?

He was making a mountain out of a molehill, he told himself. He was letting his imagination run amok and get the best of him. That had to be it.

But she inflamed him, and he wanted her.

He recalled Smash's motto "There is no love here." Boss Frank was brainwashing him but good.

#

Boss Frank took Jack into his office the next morning.

"Your production is slipping, Jack. I'm gonna have to turn you into a lamp shade."

Boss Frank blew his nose. Blood filled his handkerchief.

Jack shifted his legs anxiously in his seat. He wished he knew what Boss Frank was talking about. He looked into Boss Frank's bloodshot eyes and was at a loss. Did this little tête-à-tête have anything to do with Melody?

Boss Frank crumpled his blood-soaked handkerchief and tossed it over his desk and onto the floor beside Jack's chair leg.

"Come clean, Jack, and maybe we can work something out to our mutual satisfaction."

"I don't know what you're talking about."

Boss Frank sighed. "Do you think we're stupid here? We've had you under surveillance, because we've got you pegged as a troublemaker."

"What sort of trouble do I make?"

"You're a loner. You don't socialize with your fellow workers. What the hell are you up to?"

Boss Frank scratched his ear, and a thread of blood wended its way down his lobe then down his thick neck.

"My private life isn't any of your concern," said Jack.

"Whoever told you that lied." Boss Frank got to his feet and walked to his office window. He returned to Jack. "We understand you're seeing a married woman. Where I come from, that's called adultery."

"That's a bald-faced lie!"

"What? It's not adultery?"

"It's not happening, period."

"We have videotape that says otherwise."

"It's fake."

Boss Frank smiled. He was unfazed by Jack's denials.

"We've got the goods on you, Jack. If you don't play ball with us, we'll expose you to the world. Nobody'll hire an adulterer like you after we get through dragging your name through the mud."

"Get to the point," said Jack, feeling feisty, even though he knew Boss Frank had him over a barrel and it would behoove him not to antagonize the short-tempered Frank.

Boss Frank sat down and leaned back in his swivel chair.

He said, "I used to work for a top-secret department in the CIA. Sort of like Sidney Gottlieb's technical services department back in the seventies. You know, MK/ULTRA—brainwashing by means of LSD. The workers in my department were fired by the Agency, who shut down our department."

"Why? And why should I believe any of this?"

"The infighting petty bureaucrats in the Agency didn't want my department bathing in any of their glory, so they went behind my back and cut off our funds."

"Why are you telling me your life story?"

Boss Frank glared at him with red eyes.

Jack cringed. Boss Frank was a sight to behold, what with his red eyes and blood-streaked face and neck.

"We were involved in mind-control drugs in my department," said Boss Frank. "We made a lot of headway in that area—too much, I guess. We stepped on toes, stole a jealous colleague's thunder, and had to be stopped."

Jack glanced at Boss Frank's bloody handkerchief on the floor. "Did you sample your own product?"

"And I sampled the antidote to the mind-control drug, too. The antidote, I might add, has not been perfected. Our money was cut off before we could complete our testing."

"And you want my sympathy?"

"I want to perfect the antidote before I die from this crap they injected me with. I need you to deliver me a shipment of drugs from Mexico."

"Why should I?"

"Do you see that lamp on my desk?"

Jack looked at the indicated lamp that had a beige shade. "Yeah."

"Do you wanna look like that?"

Jack closed his eyes and shook his head. "Am I missing something here?"

"Remember your buddy Marvin?"

"Yeah."

"Haven't seen him lately, have you?"

"No."

Boss Frank pointed at the lamp shade. "That's what's left of the goldbricker. The only part worth saving. His skin."

Jack felt sick. He tried to dissemble his true feelings. He had no idea if he was successful. He did not want to give Boss Frank the pleasure of wallowing in another person's misery.

"I see we're on the same page now," Boss Frank went on. "And, of course, I'll tell everyone about your adultery—if you don't cooperate, that is."

All of a sudden it hit Jack out of the blue. Had Melody been working for Boss Frank? Had she set Jack up? Or was she an innocent bystander caught up in this quagmire?

Boss Frank withdrew a palm-sized object from his trouser pocket and showed it to Jack. It was a tan purse.

Boss Frank smiled. "I made this out of his scrotum." He opened it up. "It's for my lucky charm." It contained a rat's head.

Jack could not get out of that office fast enough. He heard Boss Frank's deep guffaws behind him, following him into the hallway like the Furies.

"O mares eat oats, and does eat oats," sang Boss Frank, still splitting his sides.

#

Now what? wondered Jack. Whatever drugs Boss Frank had dropped at the CIA had unhinged him. The man was capable of any atrocity in his current condition.

Jack had to figure out what to do. One thing was sure. He wasn't going to be Boss Frank's whipping boy.

It was time to turn the tables on Boss Frank. He had spied on Jack. Now Jack would spy on him and dig up dirt on him in the process. Turnabout was fair play. There was no way Jack could stand living like a browbeaten sheep a minute longer.

#

Jack followed Boss Frank's brand-new silver Mercedes coupe home from work that night. Boss Frank lived in a tony neighborhood in Beverly Hills. Jack wondered if Boss Frank had another source of income besides that from his delivery service.

Jack also wondered why Boss Frank, with his medical background, had gotten into the delivery business. Maybe the CIA had blackballed him from medicine as a career. Or maybe Boss Frank was so deranged he could not practice medicine anymore.

An olive-skinned guy in a 6-liter V-12 Lamborghini Diablo drove onto Boss Frank's driveway as Jack watched from his car parked on the dim-lit street.

The guy was wearing a silk moiré lemon-colored suit. He went inside Boss Frank's Spanish-styled mansion for a half hour then came out.

As he was striding to his Lamborghini in the driveway, Jack approached him.

"Frank said I could score coke off you," said Jack.

Wary at first, the guy lightened up. "You a friend of Frank's?"

"Yeah. He does deliveries for my company."

"That's Frank, all right. He delivers." The guy smirked at his obscure joke. "How much you want, my friend?"

"Does Frank got a stash inside?"

"Does a bear shit in the woods?"

"Sounds good."

"Gotta run, dude," said the guy, and ducked into his Lamborghini.

That explained Boss Frank's bloody nose, Jack decided. Too much sampling of the Colombian snowflake. And the cops would give their eyeteeth to know about Frank's stash, he was sure.

#

Jack was about to leave when he noticed a light turn on and fill an upstairs window. A man's silhouette, holding a knife or scissors, glided by the pane.

Something told Jack he should have left that minute, but he paid no heed to the warning bells that were sounding in his head.

He made for Boss Frank's front door. A cool night breeze brushed his face and harried fallen brittle brown eucalyptus leaves skittering across the driveway like so many scuttling crabs.

He tried the doorknob. It turned. Boss Frank's guest had neglected to lock it when he left.

Jack edged into the foyer, spotted the steps that led upstairs, and ascended them, trying to creep on cat's paws on the carpeted treads, fearful of alerting Boss Frank.

In the spacious corridor, Jack heard noises like muffled groans ahead of him and to his right. He made for them. The hairs on his skin stood on end. He had no idea what was going on.

Repressing an overwhelming urge to turn back, he continued forward, intent on discovering what Boss Frank was up to.

Jack cracked open the door to his right and peeked into the room, whence the groans emanated.

It was a capacious room with a table in the center of it. Nothing was out of the ordinary, except for the body lying supine on the tabletop, with its arms and legs manacled to the walnut wood.

The old man on the table, for indeed it was a man, was naked save for a bandage that covered his groin area, where his manhood used to be.

With his back to Jack, Boss Frank was hovering over the man in the ill-lit room. It was difficult for Jack to discern what Boss Frank was doing, due to the poor lighting and Boss Frank's back shielding his actions.

The nightmare scene made no sense to Jack. He could not fathom it because of its very outlandishness.

It looked for all the world like Boss Frank was carving another square on the old man's chest, which already had a checkerboard of squares tattooed on it.

Jack felt sick to his stomach. He recognized the old man who had his eyes shut in pain. It was Marvin—and he was very much alive, though in agony.

Jack took in the rest of the scene, which looked more ghastly by the second. On a straight-back chair beyond Marvin's head was sitting a stiff man dressed in an old suit. His face was covered with a black-and-white photograph of a man's bespectacled face.

As Jack was absorbing the hellish spectacle, Boss Frank turned toward him, humming the tune to *Mares eat oats and does eat oats . . .*

Jack stood rooted to the spot. Maybe Boss Frank could not make him out in the dimness, Jack hoped, even though he knew better.

Tweezers in hand, Boss Frank held up a square of skin that he had surgically removed from Marvin's chest. He deposited the bloody skin in a jar that stood by Marvin's head.

"Let the game begin," said Boss Frank.

Jack had no idea who he was talking to, if to anyone. Jack still wasn't sure if Boss Frank had twigged him. Boss Frank wasn't looking at him when he spoke.

What game? wondered Jack.

"Checkers, Mr. Gottlieb?" asked Boss Frank, as if reading Jack's mind.

Only he wasn't addressing Jack. Boss Frank was talking to the figure in the straight-back chair.

Boss Frank giggled. "Come in, Jack. I won't bite." He giggled again.

Jack could not restrain his outburst any longer. "What the hell are you going?"

"Playing checkers with Mr. Gottlieb, my idol. Isn't it obvious?""

"You're insane!"

"Don't you recognize him?" Boss Frank gestured toward the photograph taped to the seated figure's face. "Robert Gottlieb, CIA deputy extraordinaire."

"What in the world are you doing to Marvin?"

"Easy now, pilgrim," said Boss Frank, sounding like John Wayne in a B-western. "Let me explain before you have a cow. Get ahold of yourself, man." Boss Frank paused a beat, studying his handiwork on the tabletop. "What does it look like I'm doing to him?"

"It looks like you're flaying him alive!"

"Correction. I'm using his chest for a checkerboard, so I can play checkers with Mr. Gottlieb."

So saying, Boss Frank grabbed a pair of scissors and severed one of Marvin's fingers.

Marvin screamed.

"Marvin's fingers are Mr. Gottlieb's checkers," said Boss Frank in an ungodly monotone that sent chills through Jack. "I myself will use Marvin's toes as my pieces."

Boss Frank snipped off Marvin's right forefinger, punctuated by Marvin's ear-splitting cry of excruciating pain.

Jack could not stand it a moment longer. He rushed Boss Frank, not having a clear idea of what he was going to do to him when he reached him, but Jack had to do something to prevent Boss Frank from mutilating Marvin any further.

Jack crashed into Boss Frank, rocking Boss Frank on his heels and slamming Boss Frank's right hand and the scissors in it into Boss Frank's stomach.

Grimacing, Boss Frank clutched his punctured stomach. He cried out as blood percolated through his fingers and onto the scissors' plastic grip.

"Holy shit!" he wailed. "You're gonna die now, motherfucker!" he yelled at Jack.

Marvin screamed again as he saw that he was missing fingers from his right hand.

"Shut the fuck up, Checkerboard!" said Boss Frank.

With that, he stabbed at Marvin's throat with the blood-soaked scissors. His thrust missed its mark. The scissors ended up slicing Marvin's ear as Marvin flinched from the anticipated blow.

The room echoed with screams. At this point, Jack wasn't sure whose screams. Even he was screaming now, as he charged Boss Frank and leapt onto his back. The impetus of Jack's charge sent Boss Frank stumbling toward the window, Jack aboard him.

Boss Frank's face crashed through the window. Bloody glass shattered and flew helter-skelter. Jack grabbed the curtain rod and, suspended from it, tried to kick Boss Frank through the window.

Impaled on teeth of glass in the pane, Boss Frank's doubled-over body could not be dislodged, no matter how hard and how many times Jack kicked him.

At last, in frustration, exhausted, Jack stopped kicking Boss Frank's inert body that bent obscenely out the window, his massive backside facing Jack.

"Don't stop now!" howled Marvin. "Kill him! Kill him! Kick him out the window!"

Jack strode over to the seated figure and tore off its mask. He did not recognize the corpse.

"Who is it?" he asked.

Marvin tilted his head back from his supine position to eye the cadaver in back of him. "It's the founder of Smash, his father."

#

Jack heard clinking behind him. He wheeled around and spotted Boss Frank charging him and stomping on any broken shards of glass in his path. Dripping with his blood, fragments of glass jutted out of his stomach. He lunged at Jack with a foot-long spike of shattered window pane in his hand.

Jack kicked the cadaver, which fell off the chair and impeded Boss Frank.

Boss Frank stumbled and lurched to his right, slamming his head into the wall and smashing the sheetrock, which dented and crumbled raising a cloud of chalk dust.

Jack yanked a lamp's plug out of its wall socket and coiled the wire cord around Boss Frank's throat from behind.

Boss Frank winced, grabbed the wire, and tried to pull it away from his neck, choking on the chalk dust.

Jack tossed the shade off the lamp. He grasped the lamp's six-foot-high stand at the top and swung it like a baseball bat toward what was left of the window with Boss Frank tethered at the other end of the stand, still wrestling to free his throat from the wire noose.

Boss Frank blundered headlong toward the window, prodded by Jack's swing.

Jack released the lamp.

Boss Frank tumbled over the window sill and somersaulted out into the gusting, shrilling wind outside. The lamp stand sailed against the window jamb, jerked to a halt, and broke Boss Frank's fall, as well as his neck, which fetched up at the end of the wire around his throat.

Jack picked up the mangled lamp shade from the floor. "He was right about one thing."

"What?" groaned Marvin.

"He's gonna need a new lamp shade."

Going Down

"What are those stains on the trapdoor?" asked Mahoney.

"Blood."

Mahoney and the landlord of his apartment were standing in the stuffy elevator looking up at its metal ceiling as it made its creaky ascent.

"How did they get on the ceiling?" asked Mahoney.

The balding landlord scratched his ear, remembering. "A former tenant was distraught because her husband ran out on her. She was a part-time electrician. I contracted her to do work in this building, as a matter of fact. Anyway, to make a long story short, she pried open the elevator door on the sixth floor somehow and flung herself down the empty shaft."

Mahoney got the picture and grimaced. "And she landed on this roof." He glanced up again at the bloodstains.

The landlord nodded. "This car was on the first floor."

"Why don't you have someone scrub the blood off?"

"It won't come off. I've tried everything. Ajax, turpentine. Nothing works."

As the elevator continued upward, Mahoney became irritated that the landlord wasn't sweating. The mercury must have been pushing a hundred degrees and there was no air-conditioning in the cheap building. Not a drop of sweat stippled the landlord's waxlike face, whereas Mahoney was sopping wet.

They got off at the sixth floor and parted company.

Mahoney headed for his apartment, let himself in, made for the closet, and retrieved a plastic laundry basket overflowing with dirty clothes. He was angling for his apartment door when the phone rang.

For some reason, a sixth sense maybe, he thought it was his ex-wife Wendy. The very idea of her riled him and triggered a growl in his stomach. He imagined her full lips and generous head of curly honey-colored hair and became infuriated.

After he had got laid off from his job as a machinist at the bankrupt GM auto plant in Van Nuys, where he had worked for ten-odd years, she had waited a seemly amount of time–two months–before she demanded a divorce. After all, she had not married him for his fifty-thousand-dollar-a-year job.

Mahoney was sure she was already sleeping with some other guy, as like as not her lawyer. Men were always giving her the once-over.

He did not want to talk to her but maybe it was important so he set down the laundry basket and answered the phone on the fifth ring.

"Hello," he said.

He heard a beep, a few moments of silence, then a woman's sensual voice that said, "I'm not here right now but at the sound of the beep you can leave your name and phone number."

He shrugged and hauled his laundry out the door to the elevator at the end of the corridor. As he rode down the elevator it slammed against its shaft off and on, its cable wheezing under the strain of its weight.

Moments later, there was a sonorous crash as the elevator struck something hard near the second floor, sending shock waves through his legs, then continued downward. The elevator juddered and drew up in the lobby.

If the manager wasn't such a tight wad he'd have the elevator maintained, thought Mahoney on his way to the cramped laundry room, which also housed the asbestos-lagged water heater, at the north end of the lobby. You had to be an acrobat to fit into the tiny room and open and load the washer, decided Mahoney.

Contorting his body he packed his clothes in the washing machine, added liquid Tide detergent, slotted five quarters into the overpriced machine, and in surprise watched it shake and rattle as if on the verge of exploding.

"Nothing in this rattrap works," Mahoney muttered to himself.

He returned to the elevator and stepped inside it. When it rose, it shuddered and squealed like–Mahoney could not help but think it–a woman climaxing. He must have Wendy on his mind. It was that damned phone call that had started him thinking of her.

The elevator squealed again as it reached the sixth floor.

"That was good," he thought he heard a woman purr.

She must be talking to a friend in the hallway, he decided. It was like that–some days he could hear voices as he rode the elevator past floors where neighbors chatted.

But on this occasion as he left the elevator, expecting to run into a neighbor in the hall, he encountered nobody. The hallway was deserted. Then who had he heard in the elevator? he wondered.

Maybe whoever it was had split already and taken the stairs instead of waiting any longer for the elevator. Then how come he could not hear any footfalls on the stairs? He walked to the stairs, leaned over the black metal balustrade, and saw nobody on the worn linoleum steps.

Shaking off his bafflement he carried his empty laundry basket to his apartment and tossed it on the carpet. Wiping sweat off his face with the back of his hand, he missed the air-conditioning he used to have in the condo he shared with Wendy until their divorce. Now, thanks to her slick lawyer, she had the condo all to herself and he had to live in this dump so he could afford to pay her alimony with his skimpy unemployment insurance checks. What would he do when they ran out? he wondered.

He did not want to think about it.

He went to the kitchenette and drank a glass of water.

The phone rang.

On the third ring he picked up the handset and said, "Hello."

"Hello, James." This time it *was* Wendy. And he knew it was bad news, since she called him "James," not "Jim," only when she had bad news for him.

"Hi, Wendy," he said, without any inflection in his voice, he hoped. If she sensed he did not want to talk to her she would never leave him alone.

"What's wrong with the mail?"

"I don't know." He knew what she was driving at.

"I haven't got your alimony check in the mail yet, James."

"Your greedy lawyer boyfriend is richer than I am. Get it from him." He was trying to restrain his anger but it was difficult. "How long did it take you to seduce him?"

"Why are you so upset?"

"I'm not. Hey, what's the difference between a dead lawyer in the road and a dead snake in the road?"

"I don't know," she said and yawned.

"The dead snake has skid marks in front of it."

"You sound angry."

"I'm not." He knew what she was trying to do. She was a pro at it. She was trying to manipulate him by putting him on the defensive, by making him feel guilty. He wanted no part of it.

"Yes, you are, James. Now calm down and tell me why you haven't mailed me my alimony check yet."

Mahoney felt like slugging her spang in

those full lips of hers, those beautiful lilac lips. They really did look lilac, like flesh when it's cold– or dead. They were a tip-off to her cadaverous personality.

Too bad he had not realized it when he first met her and then he would not have married her–or would he have gone through with it anyway? No matter how rotten and full of herself she was inside, she remained a feast for his eyes.

"James? James, are you there?"

"Yeah."

"Then can you manage to get ahold of yourself and tell me–"

A loud click on the phone line interrupted her, followed by the words, "I'm not here right now but at the sound of the beep you can leave your name and number."

Mahoney squinted in bemusement at the handset. What the hell was going on? he wondered. He heard a beep then silence.

"Wendy?" he said into the mouthpiece.

No answer. Dead silence. Not even a dial tone.

Then: another beep. It sounded like an answering machine beeping every once in a while as it recorded. At length the answering machine hung up and a dial tone ensued.

Mahoney hung up. What happened to Wendy?

As if to answer his question, the phone rang. He started at the harsh sound. He had no idea he was so keyed up. Apprehensive, he did not want to answer it. But he did–in the middle of the third ring.

"Hello?" he said, not knowing what to expect at this point.

"James, is that you?" asked Wendy.

"Yeah. Was that your idea of a practical joke?"

"What?" She sounded bewildered.

"The thing you're doing with the phone."

"What are you talking–"

"The thing you're doing with your answering machine or whatever you're doing. It isn't funny."

"I'm not doing anything with my answering machine. We were cut off. It must've been the operator."

"No, it wasn't. You're doing something with your answering machine."

"Are you crazy? Is this one of your tricks to get out of paying alimony?"

"How do you figure that?"

"You're pretending you're insane so you won't have to pay me."

Mahoney laughed. He could not help himself. She was on a roll now. "You've got to be kidding."

"You're the one who's kidding if you think you're gonna get away with pulling this stunt!"

"It's your stunt, not mine–"

And there it was again. The click and the maddening tape-recorded message telling him to leave his name and number.

"Wendy?" he said. Forget it, he decided.

He cradled the handset. He felt like unplugging the phone from its jack so she could not hagride him anymore with her dirty tricks. What did she hope to accomplish with the silly answering machine anyway? he wondered. Was she trying to drive him nuts? Where would that get her?

He glanced at the clock-radio on the bureau and realized the wash was done. He left the apartment and entered the hot fuggy elevator. Dripping with sweat, he descended in the elevator. It shuddered and squeaked as usual and he swore he heard a woman's moaning and panting and heavy breathing . . . *and maybe he was going nuts!*

Again when the elevator door opened he expected to meet a woman standing there, but again nobody was there.

Was the heat causing him to hallucinate? he wondered. Add the heat to the fact that he felt depressed because he was unemployed and divorced and you had all the ingredients necessary for a nervous breakdown.

He did not want to think about it.

He walked into the laundry room, hauled his wet clothes out of the washer, doing his Incredible Rubber Man routine, and tossed them into the drier. The laundry room felt like the hottest place in the building. Dying to get out of there, he slotted his quarters in the drier in a flash, fumbling one of them in his haste. He grumbled, found it, picked it up, and slotted it with the others.

Like the washer, the drier commenced to rattle and shake, shaking to such a degree, in fact, that it was now moving across the floor, sliding toward him as if an enraged beast was caged inside it and trying to leap out at him.

Mahoney took off and shut the laundry-room door behind him. The drier had broken loose from its moorings, that was all.

He told himself to calm down as he checked his mailbox in the lobby. Bills. Nothing else. He was so hot he was all but gasping for breath.

He decided to open the lobby's plate-glass front door to let a breeze enter the building. He tried to crank the metal door handle. Nothing happened.

In frustration he tried the handle again. Nothing doing. It was electronically locked and he could not budge it. He cursed. The manager must have locked it for what reason Mahoney had no idea.

Sweat dripped of his forehead into his eyes and stung them. What if he had an important appointment, like with a doctor? he wondered. How could he blow this building to get there on time? The manager had no right to lock this door.

Mahoney was a virtual prisoner here. He had a good mind to call the manager and give him what-for.

As Mahoney angled for the elevator he twigged an old hunchbacked man, whom he did not know. The geezer wore an Aloha shirt and baggy charcoal grey tropical wool slacks. He shambled into the lobby and put his hand on the door's handle.

Mahoney was about to call to him that it was locked when, to his astonishment, he saw the old man open the door and walk out onto the sun-gilt sidewalk.

After regaining his composure Mahoney bolted to the door and grabbed its handle. It would not budge!

How could the old man have opened it? wondered Mahoney. Did he have a key? Mahoney had not seen him use one.

Fit to be tied, Mahoney hammered his fists on the plate-glass door, trying to attract the old man's attention. The old man ignored him and shuffled away, his back toward Mahoney.

Why doesn't the codger turn around? Mahoney asked himself in white heat. It was then that he spotted the hearing aids nestled behind the geezer's ears like blood-bloated ticks.

Well, that still did not explain why the door opened for the old man and not for him, decided Mahoney. As weird as it sounded, he felt envious of the old-timer.

It must be the heat, Mahoney concluded. Yes, that was it. He wasn't going bonkers. He had to take it easy. That was all. Then he would be all right. It wasn't a good idea to overexert yourself in hundred-degree heat.

As he waited for the elevator he heard rapping on a door and, looking in the direction of the noise, he saw the laundry room's wooden door vibrating in its jamb. Something was banging on the door trying to get out, or had the drier slid all the way across the floor to the door and was now battering against it?

The banging became so intense Mahoney thought the door would fall down any second. Should he open it? he wondered.

The only thing he wanted to do was get out of there as fast as his legs would carry him. When the elevator door slid open he jumped inside the car and ascended toward his floor.

More than anything he was teed off at the fact that he could not leave this building. The sound of that woman's moaning in the throes of–there was no other way to describe it–orgasmic bliss intruded upon his thoughts.

Maybe she lived in one of the rooms near the elevator shaft, he speculated, and that explained why he could hear her in the elevator. He did not put much stock in that theory though, for no apartments abutted the elevator shaft.

As the elevator hummed upward, creaking and lurching, he heard her voice. What was she saying? He strained his ears to hear her through the electronic buzzing of the elevator.

"I . . . love . . . you," she was saying. That was what it sounded like, at any rate. Wait, he told himself. There was more. "Why"–and the voice was so faint he could hardly hear it–"don't you ever call me back?"

She must be talking on the phone, he thought.

"Leave your name and number," she went on.

"Can you hear me?" he asked. "Who are you?" What was happening to him? he wondered. Only a numskull would talk to an elevator.

"Why don't you call me back?" Her voice sounded as if it was coming from a great distance and through soughing wind at that.

The "wind" was probably the humming of the elevator, figured Mahoney. Speaking of which, it seemed to be taking forever for the elevator to reach his floor.

He heard her say, "I don't want you to ever

leave me." She must be speaking to her lover, Mahoney surmised.

He felt embarrassed overhearing her intimate conversation and felt compelled to confess to her that he was listening in.

"Hello?" he said.

Why didn't she answer him? he wondered.

He cleared his throat noisily. "Hello."

No answer. She must not have heard him, he decided.

"I'm never going to let you leave me," she said. The elevator shuddered violently. "You make me so hot every time you enter me."

X-rated, thought Mahoney. *This is getting steamy.*

"I can hear you," he said. Maybe she would not talk so loud if she knew a stranger was eavesdropping.

"I can't stand it when you're not inside me."

If anything, she was talking louder, Mahoney decided. Maybe she got off letting strangers overhear her pillow talk. Was this elevator ever going to stop?

"Hello?" he called again.

"Every time you enter me I shudder with delight."

"I can hear what you're saying," he insisted.

"You're never going to leave me again."

"Who is that?" He whirled around, casting about the elevator for the origin of the voice.

"If I can't have you no one can."

"Hello?" Could she hear him? he wondered.

The elevator stopped.

It was about time, decided Mahoney in a

rush to get out.

However, the door remained shut. "Hell," he said.

All he needed now was for the elevator to break down while he was in it. What else could go wrong? Talk about a day when you never should have gotten out of bed . . .

He reached for the control panel and flicked the red plastic emergency switch. No soap. The door did not open. Now what? His palms felt clammy and sweat was pouring down his face into his eyes and mouth.

Looking up at the ceiling he caught sight of the bloodstained metal trapdoor. A means of escape. He could not reach it. He would have to jump to touch it. He balled himself into a crouch, sprang up, and jammed his hands against the trapdoor. It did not yield so much as a fraction of an inch.

"Ouch!" he howled as pain shot through his hands. He landed with a jolt back on the floor, shaking his sore hands at his sides.

The trapdoor felt like it was welded shut. What was that sound? he wondered. *Patter, patter*. With mounting horror he noticed blood impinging on his wrist. He looked up at the ceiling, where droplets of fresh blood appeared to ooze out of the seams around the trapdoor.

"I don't like Wendy," said the voice, distinct now, without the elevator's humming to interfere with it.

Whoever she was, Mahoney was astounded by her proximity. What did she say? he wondered. She had said "Wendy." How could she know

Wendy?

"I love you," said the voice.

"Are you talking to me?" he asked, finding that hard to believe. Was he hearing voices, cracking up?

"I want you inside me forever."

He raked the elevator for signs of a microphone. "Is this somebody's idea of a joke?" he snapped. "Let me out of here!" He fell to pounding the steel walls with his fists. The metallic echoes resounded through the compact car, deafening him.

"You make me shudder," she said huskily.

"Let me out!"

"Do it faster! Yes, there! There!"

He spun around the elevator wondering where the voice was coming from, his head becoming dizzy. The walls were swimming before his eyes, coalescing into a kaleidoscopic frenzy.

"Who are you?" he demanded as he ceased spinning so he would not lose his balance and topple over. "Let me go!"

"Never. You're mine forever."

White-faced, he felt his stomach turn over as he heard the whip-crack of a cable snapping above him and felt the elevator free-fall with a whir. He was sure he was going to faint.

He searched in desperation for something to grab, but, on second thought, what was the point?

I'm imagining this! he thought. *It can't be happening!*

"Forever! Oh yes!" she cried. "Yes!"

Dead to Rights

I wanted out of the Machine. This would be my last kill for them. I had had enough.

They were turning me into a robot. I felt lobotomized, mindless, incapable of making an independent decision, incapable of running my own individual life.

On account of them and their incessant domination of my life, I had no idea what to do with myself whenever, however rarely, I had any free time.

The full name of the organization I worked for was MachineDeath.com. It was a company that I had found while surfing the Internet casting around for a job.

They advertised for job applicants who had a military background. I had fought in the Mekong Delta thirty-plus years ago. I had Special Forces' training. I was in my late forties, and job opportunities for the over-forty club were few and far between.

I showed up at the job interview, not knowing what to expect. The Machine had provided no information over the Internet about the nature of their business. It could have been selling Victoria's Secret lingerie, for all I knew.

Alex, who interviewed me, asked me what I used to do for a living. He wore a grey suit and horn-rimmed plastic-framed glasses and, in general, looked and acted like a conservative businessman.

"I was a security guard for Ames Security," I told him.

"Why did you leave them?"

"I got laid off."

"Interesting. Why did they lay you off?"

"They were downsizing."

"That all?" He gazed at me skeptically, as though he knew there was more to it than that.

"All right. I had a personality conflict with my boss."

Alex gave me a look. "That's not a problem," he deadpanned.

I didn't tell him the real reason they had canned me. They accused me of never showing up at work, spending all my time at the track. They had the gall to tell me I should join Gamblers Anonymous. My boss, Theodore Ames, could take a flying leap, as far as I was concerned.

Alex was still staring at me when he said, "MachineDeath needs employees who can take care of unpleasant people for it."

"You want muscle."

"Right. But a lot of it, if you know what I mean."

I believed I did know. "Who are these characters you want taken care of?"

Alex stopped up one of his nostrils with his thumb, leaned to his right, behind his desk, and blew snot out of his open nostril onto the floor. He reminded me of a pro football player standing on the sideline, trying to look tough with the snot-blowing routine.

Despite the business suit, I decided, Alex was not a businessman in the traditional sense. The suit was camouflage.

Some of the snot streaked his silk moiré suit, but he ignored it, and said, "These are unpleasant people who have victimized our clients."

"Who are you clients?"

"That doesn't concern you, Roland."

"My name's not Roland. It's Jim Drake."

"OK, Brake."

I didn't correct him this time. He might think I was giving him a hard time and throw away my job application. I listened, stone-faced, pretending not to have heard him mispronounce my name.

"Here's the deal," he went on. "The Machine pays you to take care of certain not-nice guys."

I sat there in front of his metal desk, thinking about his proposition.

"I gotta tell you," he said. "We like Vietnam vets here. I think you're a shoo-in if you wanna join us. Whaddaya say?"

Killing bad guys—that was what I did in Nam. Why not join the Machine? Anyway, who else was going to hire a guy pushing fifty? Employers weren't exactly pounding down my door to hire me.

"I'm interested," I said.

"That's what I wanna here."

We stood up on his cue and shook hands.

"Lookin' good," he said, smiling with his withered lips.

All nicey-nice, at the interview anyway. As soon as I got on the payroll, it was an altogether different story.

#

I sat in my rusted-and-dinged beige '69 VW Beetle now, watching the front door of Lance Baron's chichi manse in Beverly Hills, waiting for him to leave.

It was noon. My body was stiff and ached from sitting there for hours. And I had to take a leak passing bad.

Baron would be my seventeenth victim. I had a Tec-9 machine pistol secreted under my seat, illegally set on full auto.

#

Unlike my recruiter Alex, my boss at the Machine treated me like something that crawled out from under a rock in the dead of night—either that or he ignored me.

Ganzer was his name.

Whenever he saw me in one of the halls of the corporation, he did one of three things when I said hello: he either nodded smugly at me, or looked downward pretending not to see me, or walked right by me without so much as acknowledging my presence.

He must want me to suck up to him, I decided. I was trying to be courteous by greeting him. That was a mistake. He didn't want manners from me, he wanted adulation—which made it all the more difficult for me to say anything whatsoever to him.

Ganzer was stocky, about five-ten, and, like Alex, wore a suit to work. Despite his expensive suits, Ganzer sported a cheap haircut—pretty much a garden-variety razor job from a conventional barber.

In no time, I got to the point where I could not stand seeing him. For my money, he went out of his way to make me feel inferior, like I could not exist without his stewardship.

It was all part and parcel of the Machine's grand plan—to make you feel that you could not exist as an individual, only as a subordinate extension of it, the Machine.

This feeling of valuelessness outside of the Machine was inculcated on me from day one by Ganzer and his crew of supervisor flunkies. Even inside the Machine I had little value. I was there only to carry out their orders, and my value, what little there was of it, was in carrying out those orders successfully. Beyond that, I was nothing.

Perhaps they preferred hiring job applicants with military backgrounds because military men were trained to obey orders, no questions asked. Insubordination, mutiny, was about the most heinous crime you could commit in the military.

In any case, I came to loathe the Machine and its systematic, ruthless brainwashing and dehumanizing of me, its robotization, shall we say, of me.

I had to get out of this corporation from hell or blow up.

It was dismantling me to such an extent that I could not talk to anyone on an equal footing anymore. I could not converse as a fellow human being. I felt like I needed permission even to breathe, let alone engage in companionable conversation.

In short, the Machine was driving me nuts.

Ganzer and his crew would never let up on me until I caved in and accepted as indisputable truth their dogma that I could not exist without their supervision. Pure and simple, they wanted to break me.

I refused to forfeit my individuality in order to retain a job. That wasn't going to happen. At this juncture, I sensed Ganzer realized my intransigence was here to stay. As a result, I suspected he would try to do something about it—but what?

I had no intention of finding out.

#

I caught sight of Lance Baron angling out of his house toward his custard Mercedes coupe. He was dressed casually in faded blue jeans and a grey polo shirt. Perfectly coiffed, his white hair seemed to glow in the resplendent California sunlight, setting off his rich mahogany tan. Whether it was salon induced or not, his tan enhanced his appearance.

Ganzer had told me that Baron was a plastic surgeon. From the looks of his smooth, tawny face, maybe he was one of his own patients.

Baron drove his Mercedes to a Century City mall. I followed him in my Beetle. He never once looked back at me that I could see. Why would a guy in a luxury car notice a beat-up rustbucket?

He parked in the underground garage, got out of his car, and made for a movie theater. I followed him. I wondered which movie we were going to see. I didn't have to wait long to find out.

At the theater, I looked up at the marquee. *American Psycho.* Interesting, I noted.

#

The other workers at the Machine were brainless drones. They minded their own business, said little, and did their jobs to a T, without any reservations.

They chattered about their families and their kids, etc., and seemed happy about their work. They shut up when I was around—which made me wonder, did they talk about me behind my back? Why else would they stop talking when I was around?

Maybe I was paranoid.

The Machine could make you that way easy enough if you didn't step back every once in a while, take a look at the big picture, and keep things in perspective.

There was only one other coworker who talked to me. Jack Kelvin. We hit it off at first blush. He gave me the impression that he hated this job as much as I did. With this in mind, one day, while we ate lunch at a burger joint, I asked him straight out:

"Do you like this job?"

"Are you kidding?" he said. "Ganzer runs this place like it's a Roman slave galley."

"I've had it with the Machine."

Kelvin nodded. He was older than me, in his fifties. He had cataracts on his blue eyes, and was deaf in one ear, but he got the job done. You didn't need twenty-twenty vision to off a guy.

"I'm outa here in a New York minute," he said, "as soon as I got enough moolah to quit."

"You got that right."

He squeezed ketchup on his french fries and popped them into his mouth, one at a time.

"Ganzer's a two-headed snake," he said. "Only a gelding could work for a slimebag like him. That son of a bitch leaves a trail of slime wherever he goes."

I chortled. Kelvin hated Ganzer as much as I did.

It felt good to be able to kick back and talk to a like-minded soul. Such persons were rare in the Machine.

#

Apparently I had confided in the wrong guy. The day after my conversation with Kelvin, Ganzer ordered me into his office and read me the riot act.

"How do you feel about yourself, Brake?" he asked. "Are you a winner or a loser in the game of life?"

I didn't know what he was fishing for.

"Cat got your tongue?" he said, as he shuffled papers on his desk. "I'll help you out. It starts with the letter *L*."

I didn't answer.

"What's wrong? Can't you spell either, Brake? You're a *loser*. Got it now, loser? You'd be nothing without the Machine. If we didn't hire a no-talent, no-luck loser like you, you'd be out on the streets cadging money. You're nothing without me. Less than nothing."

Maybe Kelvin had told Ganzer that I was not a happy camper, I decided. That was what I got for trusting anyone in the Machine.

"What are you trying to say to me?" I asked, humiliated.

"I thought it was crystal clear. If you don't like it here, you know where the door is."

It had to have been Kelvin, I concluded. He had ratted me out.

"OK, loser," Ganzer went on, "if you've got nothing to say, get the fuck outa here. You're polluting my air. Do your job and keep your mouth shut."

He walked over to me and patted me on the back, smiling, letting bygones be bygones.

I could not resist. I had to say it.

"Feelin' where to put the knife?" I said.

#

I never saw Kelvin again. He vanished from the corporation like he never existed. It was well and truly eerie.

Maybe his sole purpose with the Machine had been as a plant to sound me out and then expose me.

I had to be on my guard every minute. I could not put anything past Ganzer. No action was too ignoble for him to stoop to. What would he try next in order to bend me to his will, or, to be more accurate (since there were no individuals here), the Machine's will?

#

I didn't have to wait long to find out.

The next day he said good morning to me, which in itself was a surprise, as he never acknowledged me, and invited me into a nearby office.

What was this all about? I wondered.

"Sit down," he said.

I sat in a stainless steel chair that felt none too comfortable, while he remained standing.

"We're starting an IPO tomorrow," he said, puffing out his chest. "We're gonna make millions of dollars, maybe billions."

I gave him a blank stare.

"An initial public offering, you dweeb," he said. "Despite your losing efforts, the Machine's Internet stock is blasting off the NASDAQ charts. Nobody can stop us! Welcome to the twenty-first century, Brake."

I heard the door open behind me, and Alex walked into view.

"Let's start," Ganzer told Alex.

"Put your arms on the armrests," Alex instructed me.

I did so, though I didn't know what the point was.

Alex pressed a remote control in his hand, and steel cuffs snapped shut around my wrists, clamping my arms to the chair.

He pressed another button, which clamped my legs to the chair legs in the same fashion.

He removed his glasses and inserted them into the breast pocket inside his jacket. Then he reared back and drilled his fist into my solar plexus.

I gagged.

"Did you feel anything?" Ganzer asked me.

"Yes."

Alex punched me again, even harder if that was possible.

"Did you feel anything?" Ganzer repeated.

"Yes," I gasped. I felt like I would vomit any second.

Alex slammed another fist into my midriff.

"Did you feel anything?" was Ganzer's chorus.

Through waves of pain that emanated from my stomach, I managed to groan, "Yes."

What with the pain racking me and my confusion at what was happening, I could not think straight.

"Lower it," Gazner ordered Alex.

Alex pressed another button on his remote. The ceiling opened, and a transparent Plexiglas fishbowl about three feet in diameter descended toward my head.

As the fishbowl, which was filled with water, neared my head, Alex hooked up a breathing apparatus that looked like scuba gear to my mouth. Actually, it was just a hose that would allow me to breathe as the bowl of water submerged my head.

"Do you see the little fishes in the bowl?" Ganzer asked me.

I nodded. They were partitioned off from the part of the bowl that would soon ensconce my head. There were a dozen or so of them swimming about ferociously, it seemed to me.

"They're piranhas," he said.

He had my full attention.

"They'll strip the flesh off your face in nanoseconds," he went on. "The nasty little buggers are voracious. Insatiable. They'll probably go for your eyes first, eating through your eyelids, to reach the delectable jelly of your orbs. From there, it won't take them long to burrow into your minuscule brain. I'm told the human brain itself has no feeling.

"But I imagine the pain from your face being ripped off plus the pain in your masticated eyes will be excruciating. One can only wonder how much agony you'll be able to endure."

The piranhas were swimming rapidly in their end of the bowl, churning water in a frenzy, as if they sensed what was about to happen.

"If you want me to let you go," said Ganzer, "press the button in your armrest and tell me the correct answer to my question."

What the hell was he talking about? I wondered.

I had trouble concentrating on account of the shooting pain in my solar plexus that was seizing my mind and short-circuiting my thinking process.

I had to calm down and figure out the correct answer to Ganzer's question.

The bottom of the fishbowl was made of black neoprene that, when pressed down over my head, would open to allow my head to pass into the tank and yet would retain most of the water inside.

The bottom of the fishbowl did, in fact, press down over my head now.

My head was engulfed in water. I breathed through the hose. My eyes smarted in the stinging water. Everything looked blurry—including the piranhas that swam inches away from my face, the Plexiglas partition still between us. I could hardly hear Ganzer speaking on account of all that water.

"Piranhas, otherwise known as caribes, are freshwater predatory fishes found primarily in the Amazon," Ganzer was droning on. "*Caribe* is Spanish for *cannibal*. Piranhas have razor-edged triangular teeth—"

I could see the partition rising an eighth of an inch at a time. The piranhas were slamming their ugly faces against the widening aperture, sensing prey nearby, frustrated at their inability to squeeze through the crack and reach me. It looked for all the world like they were trying to chew through the Plexiglas with their prehistoric teeth.

What was the answer to Ganzer's question?

I could not stand his version of hell much longer. Weighing what the Machine in the guise of Ganzer had been doing to me day after day, my adrenaline-driven mind winging it, I thought I had the answer.

I pressed the button on the armrest, frantic to catch Ganzer's attention before the piranhas slipped through the crack into my face.

Ganzer signaled Alex to raise the fish tank from my head.

Dripping wet I coughed and spat out the hose's mouthpiece.

On the spot, Alex clenched his fist and hammered me in the stomach, putting all two hundred-odd pounds of him behind it.

"Do you feel anything?" Ganzer asked me.

I knew the answer now, because desensitization and dehumanization were what the Machine was all about. Robotization was the Machine's mantra.

"No," I answered, and they released me.

But I was lying. It was the only way to defeat the Machine—by pretending to give it what it wanted and then outwit it.

#

After *American Psycho* ended, I followed Baron to the parking garage. He drove out of his parking space, and I continued my pursuit.

As before, he paid no attention to my Beetle, even when I was but two cars behind his at the parking garage's cashier.

I handed the twentyish Iranian cashier my parking ticket. He rang up a twenty-dollar fee on the cash register.

I started. I wasn't about to pay twenty dollars for parking to see a movie.

"Do you give a discount if I saw a movie?" I asked, reluctantly surrendering a twenty-dollar bill.

"It's too late," he said. "I already rang it up."

"You do give a discount?"

I fumbled my movie-ticket stub out of my trouser pocket. By this time, Baron was long gone. How would I catch up to him?

The cashier frowned at the stub. "It's too late. I'll have to call the manager." He phoned the manager. "I already rang it up," he mumbled to me.

"I'm sorry," I said. "I didn't know about the discount."

He finished talking on the phone to the manager and handed me fifteen dollars back. "You were too late. I shouldn't give this to you. You make trouble."

"I'm sorry," I said, fed up with the guy, feeling like a wimp for apologizing over and over. It was the Machine dominating me, rendering me ineffectual in dealing with my life. *Up the Machine!* I thought.

"It'll never happen again," I apologized. "I'll never come back here again!" I snapped. "Happy now?"

He stared at me and dropped his jaw.

The only thing that mattered to me anymore was escaping the Machine. That was what I lived for.

\#

On a hunch, I drove toward Baron's Tudor-styled mansion. My hunch panned out. Baron's Mercedes was parked on his cement driveway.

I parked behind the car and approached his house's front door. I rang the doorbell.

At length, Baron himself answered the door. He had donned white shorts and was holding an aluminum tennis racket. He didn't know who I was. Why should he?

That was the whole point of the Machine— to employ killers that the victim would not fear, motiveless killers who, for that very reason, could not be traced by the police.

I had figured out what I was going to do.

"My name's Drake," I said.

"Do I know you?"

"No, Mr. Baron. I'll get down to brass tacks. Somebody put out a contract on you." I studied his face to see how he would react.

"You mean . . ."

"Yeah. You're on a hit list."

"Is this a joke?"

"It would be a pretty sick joke, wouldn't it?"

"Even if it's true, how would you know about it?"

"'Cause—" I saw his wife walk by and held my tongue. I waited for her to pass out of earshot before I continued.

"Out with it!" he said. "I'm a busy man. I haven't got all day."

I eyeballed his tennis racket. "I can see that," I said with just the right touch of irony.

"Then get on with it." He stole a glance at his gold Rolex wristwatch.

I figured it was time to tell him. "'Cause I'm the guy that was hired to whack you."

Taken aback, he froze. He looked at me like I would pull a gun on him any second.

But that wasn't my plan.

"Who hired you?" he managed to blurt.

"The company I work for handles contracts."

"That's not what I mean."

"What—"

"Who wants me killed?"

"I don't know."

"Then why should I believe you?"

"It's all done through cutouts. I never meet or know the identity of the client who puts out the contract."

"Get the fuck out of here! I'm calling the police." He wheeled toward a phone that lay on a green blotter on an antique walnut rolltop desk in his foyer. A green-shaded banker's lamp stood next to the phone.

"Wait a second," I said. "I came to cut a deal with you."

"Why should I want to make a deal with a killer, for Chrissake?"

"I could have killed you days ago."

"Then why didn't you?"

He was starting to piss me off. I told myself to take it easy. After all, I was a trained killer. I shouldn't let a rich boy's tantrum get under my skin.

"I'll make you an offer you can't refuse, Baron."

"We'll see about that. Nine-one-one is pretty easy to punch out on a phone."

"Flat out, I'm not gonna kill you."

"How sweet of you." He paused a beat. "What's the catch?"

"The thing is, if I don't take you out, another hired gun from my company will. You can bank on that. If you don't get blown away, my bosses don't get paid. They've got you dead to rights."

"What's your point?"

I sighed. "Here's my offer—"

"Finally. And the sun's still up."

I chuckled. I couldn't help it. It was sort of a funny line. "I'm offering you my services as a bodyguard."

"Why should I hire you, of all people?" He twirled his tennis racket in his hands. "How do I know this isn't a subterfuge by you to worm your way into my good graces in order to kill me?"

Not bad, I thought. He was on his toes.

"'Cause you're gonna pay me more than my present company is. I'd say five thousand dollars a month is a good round number."

"And what makes you so valuable?" He stopped twirling the racket. "Why shouldn't I just hire a bodyguard out of the Yellow Pages—somebody cheaper?"

"You get what you pay for. I know how my company's employees operate. I know how they go about scoping out a kill. I know where and when and how they like to strike. In short, I'm your best line of defense."

I could see he was mulling over my proposition. The more he thought about it, the more certain I became that I had him.

Working for Baron could not be half as bad as working for the Machine, even if he could be a prick at times.

Besides, I would not be working only for him. Once the Machine discovered that I had bolted their organization, it was a lead-pipe cinch they would go after me as well as Baron. In the end, I would be protecting both of us. And if that wasn't incentive, I didn't know the meaning of the word.

"When do you start?" he asked.

Dead Man's Hand

I didn't know how much longer I had to live.

I owed fifty large ones to Jackie the Dime and he wasn't the type of guy who had a short memory.

They called him the Dime because he did ten years in Marion for first degree murder. When he got out of the joint he was ten times meaner than when he went in. So much for rehab.

It was hot.

The humidity was so thick it seemed to drip from the sycamore leaves as I drove to Foxwoods Casino in eastern Connecticut.

I was tired of running. I wanted to end it. Running from your own shadow day in, day out was no kind of life. It was more like dying by painful degrees.

I would never be able to pay him back. *To hell with it*, I thought. Everybody died, anyway. It was just a matter of time.

In the end, death was the only thing you could count on.

Dead ahead, Foxwoods rose out of the lush verdant Connecticut woods like a mammoth blue-

and-grey French chateau. It had a cardboardlike facade with faux painted-on windows on its beveled walls.

It reminded me of a movie set on the back lot of Universal Studios, except that a movie set looked more realistic. Why paint phony windows on a building? I wondered.

Maybe they were trying to emulate the windowless look of Vegas. *The city that never sleeps*, I thought. Or maybe it was always sleeping, always dreaming—the big score, the big payoff, the jackpot that would set you free.

But this was Foxwoods, not Vegas. Was there any difference? I wondered.

I had heard Foxwoods was one of the biggest casinos in the world, if not the biggest.

Jackie the Dime wanted to meet me there. Jackie in turn, so he told me, was meeting a capo from the Partriarca family there.

That was Jackie all over—trying to impress me with his mob connections, more likely trying to intimidate me.

Whatever, I thought. I didn't need impressing or intimidation. I could not pay him what I didn't have.

I didn't know why he thought he needed to intimidate me. I had no doubt he would whack me without a moment's hesitation—if not him, one of his soldiers.

I wasn't going to worry about it. I remembered the old adage "Eat, drink, and be merry, for tomorrow we die." It sounded like good advice.

#

I parked my Pontiac Grand Am in the sprawling parking lot at Foxwoods and jumped out of the car. I was in a hurry to get out of the sweltering July heat.

Breaking into a sweat in the muggy air under the merciless sun, I strode to the casino entrance.

The sycamores bowed in the humid heat, their swollen, big, jagged leaves flush with moisture and glistening with a dewlike gloss under the raging white orb of sun.

The Mashantucket Pequot Indians ran Foxwoods on their reservation. As in most states, gambling in Connecticut was illegal, except on reservations.

I expected to see Pequot Indians employed everywhere when I entered the casino. On the contrary, I saw but a scant few.

A couple of the card dealers looked like Indians. One was dealing a poker game called Caribbean Stud, which I wasn't familiar with.

In its hugeness and its gaudiness, Foxwoods was a lot like Vegas, but I missed the girls. Nobody who looked even remotely like a showgirl or cigarette girl was present among the milling crowd.

Most of the patrons looked like retirees gambling away their pensions. They were favoring the slots.

I had close to forty dollars on me, so I would have to forgo the card games. Many of them had minimum bets of fifty dollars.

I tipped the slot attendant in one of the slot-machine rooms and asked for the location of the nonprogressive video poker machines. As I had requested, he led me to a nine/six nonprogressive machine, which, typically, had more frequent payoffs than the eight/five progressive models. I was all set.

I glanced at my watch. I could spend an hour here before my ordeal with Jackie would take place.

I sat down and fed quarters to the slot machine—one quarter for each card that I would be dealt in draw poker. The cards I drew were free.

I liked to hear the quarters rattle and clink into the tray after each hand that I won. I became mesmerized by the video poker cards spinning around in front of me, as beeps and other raucous electronic noises erupted from the slot machines surrounding mine, bearing me away to a land without care.

Time stood still.

I took off my wristwatch and jammed it into my trouser pocket. No windows anywhere. It could have been night or day, for all I knew, for all I cared.

The only things that existed for me were the whirling cards, the slot-machine cacophony, the machine's flashing lights, and the quarters that chattered as they dropped into the metal tray when I won.

The minute I won, I stuffed my winnings back into the slot to keep the frenzied activity of the machine churning.

I tossed my winnings into a milkshake-sized white wax paper cup that was provided for that very purpose.

The best I could do was to get the cup one-third filled. I went through those winnings in ten minutes. I needed more quarters.

I pressed the Change button on the slot machine. A light went on on a white plastic post above the machine.

I continued to play, using the last of my quarters, waiting for the change person. When she came, she was pushing a cart that had a white pennant that said Change on it rising above her.

She was twentyish and dark with long brunette hair. She could have been a Pequot Indian. In any event, she was cute.

I smiled at her and handed her a twenty-dollar bill. She repaid me with two rolls of quarters and left.

I tore at one paper roll like a man possessed. I clawed at it with my fingernails, struggling and cursing, trying to tear it open and get at my precious quarters.

At last I ripped it open, all but splitting a fingernail, and plunked more quarters into the slot.

I was dealt three jacks and knew I could not lose. I pumped my arm in victory at the side of the machine. My mind whirled out of control, caught up in an all-consuming dreamlike game of chance with chimerical poker cards that seemed to spin and fly into my face, hovering in midair, painting arabesques before me, almost striking my nose. I was so transported I could feel wind on my cheeks from the somersaulting of the cards in front of me in their eldritch dance.

My cell phone beeped.

"Hello," I said, annoyed at the interruption.

"Hello, Drew."

"Hi, honey," I told my wife.

"When are you coming home for supper tonight?"

"I'll be late."

"Why?"

"Business, Liz. There's nothing I can do about it." What else could I tell her? I wondered. That I was gonna get whacked by Jackie the Dime?

She sighed. "Could you bring home some coffee ice cream for Tommy when you come back?"

"Yeah. I'll get some for the kid. Don't worry. Look, I have to get back to work."

"What's that noise I hear?"

Jeez! I thought. She could hear the slot machines beeping and playing music in the background. I had to think fast. I spun lies in my mind trying to catch one that would pan out.

"That's my new CD," I improvised.

"Where are you?"

I sighed. This was getting hairy, I decided. "I'm in my truck."

"Your delivery truck?"

"Of course."

"I didn't know you had a CD player in it."

"I play it all the time." I couldn't tell if she was buying it or not. All I knew was that I had to end this conversation pronto. "I gotta run." I made to terminate the call.

"But—"

"Yes, I'll remember the coffee ice cream. Bye."

"All right. Good-bye. Good luck, honey."

Good luck, I thought. That was right. That

was all I needed. A little good luck.

I turned my cell off. To tell the truth, I thought it had been off already, before Liz rang. What was Tommy gonna do without coffee ice cream tonight and no dad to boot? I wondered.

My mind snapped back into the game in front of me. I dealt myself two more cards, but they didn't improve my hand.

I cashed out the three jacks. Quarters fell all over themselves as they plummeted out of the machine and into the tray, bouncing and sliding against the metal, eluding my right hand as it made to grasp them.

I started.

A black leather glove tapped my shoulder.

Cringing, I looked around, sensing it wasn't the change lady. I was right.

A cold-looking guy with a rough face was staring at me. He was compact, stocky, packed together like a compressed spring.

Beside him, also wearing black leather gloves, was a blonde. She looked like she must work out a lot. She was wearing a black spandex tank top that showed off her buff arms to good effect.

The guy motioned for me to stand up.

I collected what was left of my quarters, shoved them into my trouser pockets, and obliged him. He wasn't Jackie the Dime, but I was sure that Jackie had sent him. He had the look of a made guy who could handle himself.

I cut my eyes toward the gaming commission office. It was located in the front of the slots room. The office had ceiling-high plate-glass windows and I could make out a grizzled official standing inside it, inspecting reports under a green-shaded banker's lamp on his desk.

I debated whether I should signal to him to help me, to point out to him that mobsters were infiltrating the casino.

I decided against it.

It would just postpone the inevitable. Now was as good a time as any to have done with it.

My two companions beside me, I walked out of the slots room into the spacious corridor, its cathedral ceiling looming above us, dwarfing us.

On our left, the painted facades of hotel rooms rose above us, several stories high. Like the exterior of Foxwoods with its faux windows, these hotel rooms had similar phony windows, as well as phony doors, that were painted onto them. The fake doors in turn gave onto fake balconies that were merely painted onto them.

The whole effect was surreal.

Maybe I had stumbled by mistake into a Salvador Dali movie, which I was dreaming, and I would wake up any minute now if somebody would just pinch me. *Go ahead, Liz. Pinch me*—now!

But it wasn't Liz pinching me, it was the Dime's man jostling me into an elevator.

We headed to the fourth floor of the casino hotel.

Why couldn't I be satisfied as a delivery guy working for Fed Ex? I asked myself belatedly. Why did I have to borrow myself into an ever-deepening hole that was looking more and more like my grave?

#

In our windowless hotel room was a poker table with green felt on it, a deck of poker cards in the center.

Dime's soldier, who stood about five-feet-eight and allowed little emotion to play across his determined face, ushered me into the room, none too gently.

I protested.

The mobster pulled a gun on me.

I shut up.

He trained his .22 automatic on me.

The muscular blonde followed his lead. She pulled out a .22, also.

No wonder they were both wearing gloves, I decided. They didn't want to leave fingerprints on their pieces after they took me out.

"Where's Jackie?" I asked.

"I'm Burt," said Jackie's soldier.

"I could care less."

He came up on me fast. He was behind me in no time. He punched me in the kidney with a sharp jab. I staggered forward, grimacing.

"You're rude," was all he said.

I winced in pain. "I wouldn't exactly call you polite, Burt," I said between gasps, doubled over, my hand clutching my aching kidney.

"Jackie can't set foot in Foxwoods," he said. "The gaming commission would give him the bum's rush."

"He told me he was gonna be here with a guy from the Patriarca family."

"I don't care what the fuck he told you. Sit your ass at the table."

I eyeballed his gun, sat down.

"First, do you have the money?" he went on.

"No."

"Where is it?"

I shrugged. "I don't have it."

"Wrong answer."

"It's the truth."

"Then we're gonna play poker. Five card stud. For the fifty large."

"With what?"

"Do it, Samantha," he said.

She bounded in my direction and grabbed me from behind in a headlock so I could not move.

Burt withdrew Bowie knives from the inside of his sports jacket and set them in a bundle on the tabletop. He picked one up and stabbed the tabletop, then did likewise with another knife.

He snatched my right hand and, pulling my arm toward him, inserted my wrist between the two blades.

He plunged another knife into the tabletop in front of my fingers. He pulled out a string, tied it to the pinkie of my trapped hand, pulled my pinkie away from the rest of my hand with the string, and secured the other end of the string around the planted knife blade's blunt upper edge, stretching my pinkie taut on the tabletop.

Eyes bugging out, I said, "I told you, I don't have any money."

He ignored me. "These are the stakes. If you win the hand"—he chuckled at his pun—"we cancel one K from your debt."

I dreaded asking him, but I held my breath and said, "And what if I lose the hand?"

He smiled. For the first time since I had met him, he seemed genuinely happy.

"If you lose the hand," he said, chortling, "you lose a finger. Get it—fingers for hands?"

Samantha's arm around my throat, I shivered.

"Too bad you have only ten fingers, sweetie," she said.

Struggling for breath I managed to splutter to Burt, "What's that gonna prove? You're still not gonna get the money."

"Jackie the Dime will get satisfaction and respect," said Burt.

He sat down, shuffled the cards, and dealt three hands.

"Why three hands?" I asked. "There's only you and me."

"Samantha's playing too." He smiled smugly.

"I have to beat both of your hands?"

"You got it."

I wished I could wipe away the sweat that was streaming down my forehead into my eyes. On my way to the casino I had prepared myself mentally for dying, but not for mutilation.

For my money, the latter was, by far, a worse prospect. Losing one finger at a time . . . How long would it take for me to die at that rate? I wondered. Would they stanch my blood or let me bleed out? Just thinking about it was torture in itself.

"Take it out now, Sami," Burt said.

She tied my left hand behind my chair-back and walked in front of me.

I sneaked a glance at her face. She gave me a thousand-yard stare.

In response to Burt's instructions, she opened her black leather purse and removed a gleaming hatchet from it. *Not what the doctor ordered*, I thought. *Not by a long shot.*

She laid the hatchet on the tabletop. Then she fished out a bottle of rubbing alcohol and cotton swabbing, both of which she placed beside the hatchet.

Burt caught me staring at the alcohol and cotton.

"We don't want you to bleed to death," he explained. "We want this to be a long, entertaining night."

He and Sami sat down across from me. He handed her the pack of cards and picked up his gun again.

"Deal," he told her.

She dealt five card stud.

She dealt me a measly pair of sixes, which had my adrenaline pumping overtime. Nevertheless, their hands looked worse. She dealt the fifth card to us.

Burt and Sami turned over their hole cards, their faces expressionless. With relief I saw that my puny sixes were enough to win.

But how long would my luck hold? I wondered. *For fifty hands in a row? Dream on!*

"You only owe us $49,000 now," said Burt.

Samantha shuffled the cards and dealt new hands to us. I wasn't so lucky this time.

"OK, you owe us one finger," said Burt.

He snagged the hatchet in a swift,

economical movement that caught me by surprise.

I could not watch.

I shut my eyes.

"Do you have the forty-nine grand?" he asked me.

"I already told you, no."

"Too bad."

I heard a thump. After a moment, I felt agonizing pain. I could not restrain myself. I opened my eyes. I had to see.

To my horror, I saw my pinkie about three inches away from the rest of my hand, blood gushing out of the stub that remained of the digit on my hand.

Samantha poured alcohol on my mutilated hand, then pressed cotton swabbing on the wound to stanch the bleeding.

"Do you think you can stand losing nine more hands, Drew?" Burt asked me.

White-faced, nonplussed, I watched Samantha go about her business with the blood-soaked cotton swabbing.

My mouth and throat were parched. I could not have spoken even had I wanted to. My mind was swimming. I felt like I might pass out.

"You have one other choice," he said.

I looked at him in puzzlement, my twisted face pouring with sweat.

"Go ahead, Samantha," he said.

She let go of the cotton swabbing, allowing blood to spurt out of my mutilated pinkie stub. I flinched at the sight. Then she removed the glove from her left hand. Which made me flinch almost as much as did the sight of my blood pulsing out of what was left of my finger.

Taken aback, I saw that she, too, was missing her pinkie. The glove had masked her amputation.

Her face, as usual, was expressionless.

Burt held up his left hand. He slipped off his glove. His hand was in worse shape than Samantha's. All that remained on his hand was his thumb and one finger.

"I held out a little longer," he said.

"I don't get it," I squawked. "What's this all about?"

"We either go on playing or you join us."

I gave him a look.

"You become an enforcer for Jackie the Dime like Sami and me," he said. "We started out like you." He nodded at his mutilated hand that he was still holding up. "We ended up like this."

It was Hobson's choice, I decided. And both Sami and Burt, of all people, knew it.

"Welcome to the club," said Burt.

Cash's Big Night

When the kid spat blood into his face as Cash stood at ringside, Sam Cash suspected the welterweight Rafael Luz, who stood in the ring above him, might have talent.

What decided Cash was the moment he saw Luz rock his opponent's head back with a solid right hook that all but busted his opponent's jaw.

An Oscar de la Hoya Luz wasn't—not yet, anyway—but Luz had something, Cash decided. Luz was a natural boxer; it was in the way he moved, Cash could see. He could sell this guy to the boxing world, and the more Cash watched him fight, the better Luz looked.

Over and over, Cash told his buddies in the fight game how good Luz was. At first they scoffed. They had heard it so many times before from Cash. After all, they knew it was his job as a promoter to hype boxers.

Undeterred by their cold shoulders, Cash persisted in singing the praise of Luz to the boxing cognoscenti.

"You got the makings of a champ," Cash told Luz at ringside at the LA Forum one night.

"Yeah. Says who?"

"Says me."

"And just who are you?"

"Sam Cash." Cash extended his hand to Luz, who shook it. "I'm a promoter. I can make your career."

The kid toweled off the sweat on his naked chest, a slash of a skeptical sneer on his full lips.

"I'm gonna make you a world-class boxer," said Cash.

After Luz got dressed, they walked across the street under a thin smile of moon to a bodega, bellied up to the bar, and knocked back a couple of Gusano Rojo mescals.

"How does it feel?" asked Cash.

"How does what feel?"

"Knowing you're gonna be rich?"

"I don't know that."

"You know it now, because I'm the one who's gonna make you rich."

Luz nursed his mescal, looking pleased.

"I'll mange you for 10 percent of the purse," Cash said.

"Why should I choose you over some other manager?" Luz pronounced *manager* "manaher."

"How many of them have told you you're the best boxer they've ever seen?"

Luz shrugged.

"That's my point," Cash went on. "I believe in you. I believe you have what it takes to become the next champ."

"I don't know."

"You don't know what? You don't know if you are the next champ? I don't want to hear that.

Never doubt yourself, or you'll always be a loser."

"I don't know if I want you for my manager."

Cash sighed. He took a swig of his mescal. "Like I said, you need a manager who believes in you. I'm that guy. You got the talent, and I got the contacts."

"Are you sayin' I should quit my day job? I got a wife and a *niño* to support."

"What's your day job?"

"I'm a dish washer."

"No doubt about it—quit. You do want to be rich, don't you?"

"Yeah. Like everybody else."

"Except everybody else can't box like you. You got the gift. I know this business like the back of my hand, and, believe you me, you got it."

"OK. I'm in." Luz reached out his hand toward Cash.

"Deal," said Cash, and consummated it with a handshake.

Luz drank from the bottle of mescal and like to gulped down the worm at the bottom of it.

"How many fights you been in?" asked Cash.

"Three."

"So, you're three and 0," Cash mused out loud.

"Not exactly."

Cash started. "I can't believe you lost a match."

"The son of a bitch head-butted me and cut open my eye. I wanted to pull a Tyson on him and chew off his ear."

Cash nodded. "He knew it was the only way he could beat you." He paused a beat. "Two knockouts, then?"

"One—and one TKO," Luz added hastily.

Cash smacked his lips. "I knew it."

#

Cash drove home to his wife Barbara in Alhambra and gleefully told her about his new prospect Rafael Luz in the living room of their pink stucco bungalow.

"Don't, Sam," she said dryly and turned away from him.

She snatched a leather leash off a metal hook screwed to the back of the front door and clipped the leash to her Golden Retriever's collar.

The dog whined, then wagged his tail, looking up expectantly at her.

"I'm taking Goldie for a walk," was all she said without looking at Cash, as she opened the door.

"Come on, honey," urged Cash.

But she said nothing and didn't look back as she walked down the cement path that cut through the front lawn to the sidewalk.

A couple of moths swirled into Cash's face as he stood framed in the doorway.

#

Later that night, Cash went to the manager of the number-three contender for the welterweight crown and chatted him up.

"I got a guy that can stand toe to toe with your man Rattler Rodriguez," Cash told Bill Amici, "and then knock his brains out."

Sitting behind a cluttered desk in his equally cluttered office, the white-haired Amici didn't blink his blue eyes. They could have been spheres of ice set in his craggy face for all the emotion he displayed.

"I wish I had a dollar for all the times you've told me that, Cash. I could retire a rich man."

Cash did a little dance in front of Amici's desk, working himself up for his hard sell.

"My guy, Rafael Luz, is dynamite," said Cash. "In fact, that's what I call him—Kid Dynamite."

"Catchy name," Amici said and rolled his eyes in disgust.

"I'm tellin' ya, he's world-champ*een* material."

"Who?"

"Rafael Luz."

"Never heard of him."

"The kid's got twenty fights under his belt–all KOs."

Amici raised his caterpillar eyebrows. "Not bad. So why haven't I heard of him?"

"Because he's got enemies. Everybody's jealous of him."

Amici snickered. "*Puh*-lease. What's the real reason?"

Cash relaxed. "Beats me. Maybe 'cause you don't want to know there's a guy out there that can go mano a mano with the Rattler."

"You're shittin' me."

"I kid you not. Rafael Luz is the Real

McCoy."

Amici picked up the wet remainder of a smoking cigar from a cut-glass ashtray and munched on the saliva-soaked butt, rolling it around in his mouth as he spoke.

"So, you finally hit the big time, huh, Sam, or is that what you want me to believe?"

"Take my word for it, Bill. Luz is a contender."

Amici shook his head. "Sam . . . Sam . . ."

"What is it? Are you scared I'm right? Are you scared everybody's gonna find out Rattler's nothin' but a jumped-up, hyped-up no talent?"

Amici bolted to his feet, kicking his chair so far behind him that it struck the wall. "You got the gall to say that to me, you two-bit bottom-feeder!"

"If the shoe fits . . . ," Cash trailed off.

"Rattler would wipe the floor with your bum."

"Put your money where your mouth is."

"You wouldn't know a decent fighter if you saw one. You don't know shit from shinola." Amici leaned his fists on the desktop. "You're a nobody, Sam, a big-mouth nobody. And that's why you don't have a single good boxer and never will. 'Cause all you got is a mouth the size of Texas."

"You're scared, Bill. 'Fess up. You're scared Kid Dynamite would knock your boy Rattler clear out of the ring in the first round."

Amici guffawed. "All right, Blowhard, you want to be taught a lesson?"

"Yeah, Professor Amici."

"Don't push it, Sam."

"All I want is a boxing match."

"This what's-his-name—"

"Rafael Luz."

"Yeah. He better be as good as you say he is."

"Mark my words, Bill, he *is* a contender."

Amici waved his hand dismissively. "I'll see if I can scare something up."

#

As he left Amici's office, Cash told himself over and over that for once in his life he had a winner on his hands. He strode down the avocado-painted corridor, full of vitality. He felt like he could take on the world.

Luz was Cash's ticket to the good life and Cash knew what he had to do next.

So what if he was, like Amici had said, a nobody—a five-foot-seven nondescript, fortyish nonentity that nobody looked at twice. That was all about to change, decided Cash, when he hit the jackpot with Luz's upcoming fight with the Rattler.

Cash's next move was to set up a meet with Vincent.

#

According to the IRS, Vincent Caparelli did not exist. He had never paid taxes in his "nonexistent" life.

Cash did not know Vincent's occupation, and Vincent would not have told him even if Cash had had the nerve to ask.

All Cash knew about Vincent and all he cared to know was that Vincent handled bets on boxing matches. He was responsible for handling large sums of money that were laid down by fat-cat bettors.

Cash met a reluctant Vincent in a dim-lit nude bar near the Forum.

As Guns 'n' Roses' "Welcome to the Jungle" blared from the surrounding loudspeakers, strippers pranced around on the stage looking bored or exhausted or both. Cash could not tell which.

"There's one thing I can't stand," Vincent told Cash in a low matter-of-fact voice at the back of the barroom where the music wasn't so overpowering.

Just sitting across from Vincent gave Cash the willies. Cash wondered how he had gotten on Vincent's bad side without even opening his mouth yet.

"What's that?" asked Cash.

"I can't stand having my time wasted." Vincent clasped his thick-boned quarterback's hands on the tabletop.

"You're gonna thank me when I tell you—"

"Cut to the chase."

"Rafael Luz is gonna clean Rattler Rodriguez's clock in the ring."

"Rafael who?"

"Luz."

"Luz, as in *loser*? I never heard of him, and I don't like that name."

"I'm changing his name to Kid Dynamite."

"How come I never heard of him?"

"I've kept him under wraps. This kid's got thirty KOs under his belt and not a single loss."

"Not bad."

So what if he was exaggerating Luz's record

a tad, Cash told himself. For sure, Luz was good for at least thirty KOs.

"He's a natural-born champ," said Cash. "Smart money bets a bundle on him and cleans up. Nobody will expect this unheard-of kid from TJ to dethrone Rattler."

"How do you know so much about this Lose guy?"

"I'm his manager. I found him—a diamond in the rough." Cash smiled.

"He sounds pretty good. How could you have kept him secret for so long?"

"Nobody else has my eye for spotting talent. I'm not the new kid on the block. I've been around awhile."

"Not to put too fine a point on it, your track record speaks for itself."

Cash bridled. "What do ya mean?"

"I mean, all your other boxers sucked."

Vincent's tone disconcerted Cash. He felt like he should apologize to Vincent for annoying him. Cash explained himself. "Play the hand you're dealt."

"You sound like a fuckin' fortune cookie. Spit it out so I can understand it without a translator."

"I never had a good boxer to work with. This is the first time that a champion has walked into my life."

"Then how do you know?"

"Know what?"

"Know that he's any good—if you never saw a champ before."

"I seen champs! I just never had one in my

stable."

Vincent ordered a beer from the waitress. "I hate to tell you this, Cash, but you got a reputation built on mud." He half-smiled at Cash, gloating.

Cash wanted to tell him to shove it, but bit his tongue. Vincent was a made guy, he knew.

Vincent went on, "Why should I believe you about this what's-his-face?"

"I know talent when I see it. To my trained eye, Luz is in a league of his own."

"The heavy hitters were planning to bet a couple hundred K on Rattler for his next fight."

"That's why I'm telling you to bet on Kid Dynamite. He's a lock bet. You can't lose. I wanna put down money on him myself."

Vincent didn't beat around the bush. He looked Cash straight in the eyes and said, "Bill Amici says you're a bullshitter. He says he's gotta wear boots around you so he doesn't step in it."

"Bill Amici's a bullshitter."

Vincent sniggered. Then he stretched his arms over his head. "I hope, for your sake, you're right."

"Bet the ranch, Vincent. You'll see. Luz is *that* good. It won't even be gambling."

"Because if you're wrong," Vincent said. He leaned toward Cash and planted his elbows on the tabletop without saying anything. He merely jutted his set visage inches from Cash's face.

#

Cash walked two blocks to the gym and watched Luz spar with a bush leaguer.

Luz didn't look too sharp, Cash decided.

Maybe he was having a bad day. Even the best had bad days once in a while. And Luz was the best, Cash was sure of it.

#

Then the phone calls began at Cash's house:

"If you're setting me up, I'm gonna cut off your balls and hand them to you in a glass." *Click.*

It didn't matter who it was, Cash decided. He had expected them. Life was cheap when scads of moolah were at stake.

These same callers, he knew, would be falling all over themselves trying to pat him on the back after they won their bundles of dough.

#

On the big night, Cash, sitting in the second row, could not believe it when Luz fell to the canvas in the first round.

Cash cheered him on as Luz stumbled to his feet. The referee wiped Luz's gloves off on his shirt and pointed him in the Rattler's direction.

Luz's mouth was bleeding as the Rattler hammered it with a roundhouse right, then connected with a sharp left uppercut to the jaw. Luz staggered around the ring on rubber legs.

"Nail him, Rafael! Nail him!" Cash cried as he sprang to his feet and cupped his hands in front of his mouth. *Of all the times for Luz to have a bad night*, he thought.

Thirty seconds later, it was over. Luz lay on the canvas in a bruised bloody pile of lifeless meat, his swollen face unrecognizable.

"He never touched me," crowed the Rattler,

cavorting around the ring, pumping his fists high over his head, exulting in his victory.

Taken aback, Cash could do nothing but watch.

Most of the audience booed the brief mismatch of a fight.

"Refund! Refund!" a bald, tattooed man behind him jeered. "Kid Dynamite's not even a firecracker!"

Catcalls and raspberries rained down on the ring.

Cash felt humiliated. He bowed his head. When he moved to leave, he felt as if myriad eyes were glaring at him, condemning him for being such a fool.

He spotted Bill Amici in the crowd. Amici commenced laughing his head off at him, the fat wet cigar falling from Amici's mouth.

Cash made his way up the aisle as if trudging through quicksand. He was surprised to see Luz come up to him from behind. They exchanged looks.

"You embarrassed me," Cash muttered to the bloody misshapen face.

Luz opened his mouth, and blood streamed out of it.

"You made me a laughingstock," said Cash.

"You low-rent bullshitter!" Amici called to him. "You got what was coming to you! You nobody!"

"You made a monkey out of me," Cash told Luz.

"Wake up, little man!" cried Amici. "You're nothing! What's the matter? Did you start to believe your own lies? Ha-ha-ha! You're an even bigger fool than I thought!"

Cash broke away from Luz, trying to distance himself from the disgrace that Luz had heaped on him. Cash accelerated his pace.

Then he saw Vincent up ahead.

He was standing in the aisle watching him with stony eyes. Cash's heart skipped a beat. He froze. He turned over what to do. He had no choice. There was nowhere to hide. He continued to walk. Anyway, decided Cash, Vincent wouldn't risk doing anything to him in front of all these witnesses. Would he?

"Luz embarrassed me," Cash croaked to Vincent, through a dry throat.

He expected Vincent to follow him out into the alley, but Vincent did a strange thing. He stood there and cracked a smile of disgust at Cash.

"You dime-store phony," said Vincent. "You don't really think I believed a fuckin' word you told me, do ya? Do I look like I just got off the boat?"

"You didn't bet on Luz?" Cash asked with relief.

Vincent smirked, shook his head, and walked away.

Oswald's Gun

Lee Harvey Oswald assassinated President John F. Kennedy on November 22, 1963, in Dallas, Texas, with a 6.5 mm Carcano rifle, also known as a Mannlicher-Carcano.

The question the CIA wanted answered forty-odd years after the fact was, who hired Oswald? As far as they were concerned, that question had never been answered to their satisfaction.

They ordered the independent contractor hit man Brad Jackman to find the answer.

Jackman, an ex-Marine sharpshooter pushing fifty, knew a thing or two about weapons. On being assigned the job by the CIA, he had studied the Warren Commission report on the Kennedy assassination and had gleaned numerous details about Oswald's rifle.

For instance, Oswald's Carcano bore several inscriptions on it, including "CAL. 6.5," "1940," "MADE ITALY," and the serial number C2766.

Oswald fired three 6.5 mm copper-jacketed round-nosed bullets at Kennedy. The 6.5 × 52 mm Italian Carcano M91/38 bolt-action rifle had an

Ordnance Optics 4 × 18 telescopic sight mounted on it and contained a six-round magazine.

"Who provided Oswald with the rifle?" asked Mason Kingsley, the deputy director of operations at the Agency, over the phone to Jackman, who stood in a phone booth at LAX Airport. "That's the question."

"He bought it for himself, didn't he?" said Jackman, recalling what he had read in the Warren report.

"That's what we were led to believe— erroneously."

"And now over forty years later, somehow we know the answer," said Jackman, irony intended.

"If it wasn't for your lip, Jackman, you might be more than an independent contractor for us and eligible soon for a Company pension."

Jackman ignored Kingsley's barb. "So who bought the rifle for Oswald?"

"Our informant hasn't told us yet. He's going to tell you."

"When?"

"Tomorrow in Vegas."

"Where do I meet him?"

"He didn't say yet."

"Great," Jackman sighed.

"He's going to call you at your hotel room at the Venetian. We gave him your room and telephone number there."

Jackman was about to reply when Kingsley hung up.

Jackman swore under his breath and followed suit.

An instant later the phone rang. Jackman picked up circumspectly. "Hello?"

"And don't blow it, like you did the last assignment," snapped Kingsley. "Let this guy talk before you waste him."

"Am I supposed to waste him?"

"You are a hit man, aren't you?"

"My last gig? Are you talking about the Juarez hit?"

"Yes, your last 'gig,' as you so quaintly put it." Kingsley said "gig" as if the word nauseated him.

Jackman winced at Kingsley's snide remark. They didn't call him Snarky Kingsley behind his back at headquarters at Langley for nothing, decided Jackman. Actually, it was one of his kinder epithets.

Kingsley went on, "You were supposed to pump that al Qaeda terrorist there in Mexico in an extraordinary rendition before you blew him away."

"He was trying to kill me, for Chrissake."

"Details," Kingsley scoffed. "If you botch this gig, you're on your own. I never heard of you."

"Have you ever worked in the field? It takes split second timing to make a decision. He pulled a gun on me—"

Kingsley cut him off. "I don't have the time."

"Why did you tell me to bone up on Oswald's rifle?"

"You'll find out."

"I don't get—"

"And don't have another one of your episodes."

"Episodes?"

"That you're being followed all the time. Paranoia, that is."

"You know what Henry Kissinger said: even paranoids have enemies."

"You have at least one."

Jackman heard Kingsley laughing as he hung up, again. Jackman slammed the handset into its cradle.

Smarmy Yalie thinks he knows everything, thought Jackman.

#

Jackman's Boeing 737 touched down at McCarron Airport in Las Vegas in less than an hour after taking off from LAX in Los Angeles.

He boarded a shuttle that headed to the Venetian on the Strip.

He entered the Venetian, a grandiose structure modeled after an Italian palazzo, half an hour later. Four gondolas were sitting empty and tied with painters in the placid turquoise canal in front of the Venetian.

He told the bald concierge his name and checked into the room that Kingsley had reserved for him.

Realizing he needed money he rode the elevator to the lobby and located an ATM. Somebody had beat him to it.

The man looked familiar, decided Jackman. In fact, it looked like him, Brad Jackman himself in the flesh! The same height, the same build. However, Jackman couldn't make out the man's countenance. The man continued facing away from him as he took leave of the ATM.

Jackman rubbed his chin in reflection and approached the now-deserted ATM. How bizarre, he decided, to see someone who looked so much like yourself. He inserted his magnetized bank card and punched in his PIN.

Nonplussed, he gasped at the computer screen. He couldn't believe his eyes. The terminal said his account was frozen. *Access denied.*

What was going on? he wondered. Was this Kingsley's handiwork? *That bastard!*

Jackman inserted his card again, with the same results.

Fit to be tied, he returned upstairs and used the land line in his room to call Kingsley.

"Hello?" answered the neutral voice.

Jackman could see Kingsley's middle-aged face now, the stone-washed blue eyes, the shapeless tenuous mouth with the barest suggestion of a sneer on it.

"What's going on, sir?" said Jackman, trying to restrain his anger.

"Don't tell me. Let me guess. You iced him already?"

"Listen to me. My bank account's frozen. Is this your doing?"

"Are you kidding?" Kingsley mocked. "Why would we do that?"

"You tell me."

"I'll tell you to leave me alone and don't call me again till you've got the goods from our informant."

"How am I supposed to get any money?"

"Ask me if I care."

That was the end of their conversation.

Jackman didn't know what to make of it. He could think of only one thing to do. He called his bank and told his problem to the customer service rep.

She told him to wait on the line while she accessed his bank account.

She got back to him five minutes later. "Your account's frozen, Mr. Jackman."

"Tell me something I don't know. But why?"

She hung fire.

"Hello?" he said.

"Yes. According to our records, you already made three withdrawals from an ATM today. That's your limit. You can't make another withdrawal for the rest of today. I'm sorry, but it's bank policy."

"I haven't made three withdrawals today. I haven't even made one."

"OK. Take it easy. We'll clear this up for you."

She asked him two security questions—his social security number and his mother's maiden name.

"Excellent," she said in response to his answers. "I'll double-check your account."

"Obviously there's been a mistake."

"Our records clearly state that you made three withdrawals today from an ATM."

Jackman's patience was wearing thin. "Where supposedly did I make these withdrawals?"

"Let's see. From an ATM in the Venetian Hotel in Las Vegas."

Jackman stood frozen to the spot, his hand clenched tight around the handset.

"That can't be," he managed to mutter at last.

"Why not, Mr. Jackman? Where are you calling from?"

"From the Venetian," he said under his breath, hating to admit it.

"Your account will be accessible tomorrow," she said politely. "Is there anything else I can help you with today?"

"I didn't make any ATM withdrawals today," he protested.

"Our records indicate—"

Jackman hung up in frustration.

Somebody was impersonating him, he decided. Of that much he was certain. It might indeed have been the man resembling him that he had seen at the ATM moments before using it himself.

Was he losing his mind? Jackman wondered. No. Somebody had accessed his account at a Venetian ATM. The bank confirmed three withdrawals by him. Who was doing it? And how? Why?

His overheated mind was giving him the mother of all headaches. There was nothing for it. He would have to wait till tomorrow to withdraw money from his account.

He all but jumped out of his shoes as the phone rang.

"Yeah?" he answered warily.

"Is this Brad Jackman?"

"Yeah. Who's this?"

"Your boss told me to contact you."

"Is this about Oswald?"

"I don't want to talk about it over the phone."

"Where?"

"Let's meet in the restaurant in the casino. The Grand Lux Café in ten minutes."

"I don't know what you look like. How—"

The man hung up.

#

At the Grand Lux Café Jackman gave his name to the smiling twentyish hostess and asked for a table for two. She led him to a crowded banquette.

He forked over a ten-dollar bill to her and said, "Could we have a little more privacy?"

She nodded, accepted the tip, and ushered him to a deserted table in the back of the restaurant.

He thanked her as she provided him with two menus. He ordered a Corona longneck.

Five minutes later a man about five feet eight approached his table and said, "Jackman."

It wasn't a question.

The guy was already in the process of sitting across form him when he said it.

"Mr. . . . ?" said Jackman

"Just Joe."

Joe was sporting a de rigueur three days' growth of blue-black stubble on his pie face. Clad in a khaki racing jacket and jeans, he fit right in with the casually dressed clientele at the restaurant.

His one remarkable trait was a facial tic at

the corner of his right eye to complement his head's slight tilt in that same direction. A man with disturbing thoughts eating at him? wondered Jackman, interpreting the tic.

"What's the dope on Oswald?" asked Jackman.

"What do you know about him?"

"The usual. He killed JFK."

"On his own?"

"You mean the Grassy Knoll Theory? That there were other gunmen?"

"No. I mean somebody hired him to waste Kennedy."

Jackman nodded, remembering the assassination. "Oswald said he was a patsy."

"That's one way of putting it. He did kill Kennedy, though." Joe leaned across the tabletop closer to Jackman. "I've discovered who hired Oswald to do it."

"I'm all ears."

Joe withdrew cherry-flavored Chapstick from his trouser pocket and applied the red balm to his lips with three deft swipes of his hand.

"The Crescent Firearms, Inc." he said, "distributed the assassin's Carcano rifle to Klein's Sporting Goods Company. According to the Warren Commission, Oswald ordered the Carcano by mail and received it at PO box 2915 in Dallas."

"Where are you going with this?" Jackman interrupted.

Joe waved his hands in front of him, signaling Jackman to be patient. "The rifle was mailed to A. Hidell, not to Oswald, at Oswald's PO box."

"Oswald used an alias."

"The Warren Commission mistakenly concluded that Oswald ordered the rifle from Klein's. I've found out the truth."

"And?"

"A. Hidell did order the Carcano, but 'A. Hidell' wasn't an aka for Oswald this time. It was an aka for someone else."

"Two guys are using the same alias. Hard to believe."

"The aka 'A. Hidell' was also used by the Chicago mobster Sam 'Momo' Giancana."

Jackman straightened in his seat. "Are you saying Giancana hired Oswald to kill Kennedy?"

"Giancana had the motive. JFK's brother Bobby, the attorney general, was making life miserable for the Mafia."

"A lot of people had motives to kill Kennedy. The Soviets, for one. And Oswald spent time in the USSR."

"JFK was fooling around with Giancana's mistress Judith Exner. Giancana got jealous. JFK had to get whacked."

"Do you have any proof of this?"

"I have a document proving that Sam Giancana used the alias 'A. Hidell.' And A. Hidell's signature is on the check that paid for Oswald's rifle. What more proof do you need?"

"Where's the document?"

"Upstairs in the safe in my room," Joe said sotto voce.

"You're saying there was a conspiracy to kill Kennedy."

"Managed by the puppet master Giancana.

And there's a conspiracy to cover it up to this day."

"Why? That was over forty years ago."

"A honcho in the government was also involved in the conspiracy."

"Who?"

"I'm working on that. I have reason to believe—"

Joe never finished his sentence.

His head jerked forward then back as a hole exploded between his eyes. Blood gushed out onto the tablecloth, splattering Jackman's face and the front of his shirt.

Jackman recoiled in shock. He hadn't heard a sound. A silencer was being used, he decided.

A hole appeared in the banquette behind him next to his left shoulder. Hunching his shoulders he ducked to his right to exit his seat and bolted for the front door of the restaurant. He still didn't know where the bullets were coming from.

He sprang into the casino that skirted the restaurant, knocking customers out of his way as he made good his escape.

Rock music, a song by Aerosmith, was pounding through the casino from a stage off to his right where a rock band played in spotlights, the band members' faces awash with neon purple that percolated from the high intensity bulbs.

To dodge bullets he jinked through the casino and arrived at the main staircase that swept down grandly from the second floor.

He fled up the stairs. The cathedral ceiling above him looked like something out of the Sistine Chapel with its knots of paintings mantling it. The religion in Vegas wasn't about God, it was about money. Instead of cathedrals that vaulted to the heavens, graced with artwork; grandiose casinos arched upward to touch the sky, clad in ersatz Leonardo da Vincis and Michelangelos.

Jackman bucketed up the stairs to the Grand Shoppes that lined the winding indoor canal. The roof was a canopy that mimicked the azure sky.

He whipped past the chichi boutiques along the canal. Gondolas floated aimlessly in the still water, the gondoliers crooning as they poled their boats forward.

Jackman paused at a jewelry store just long enough to look back, casting around for the murderer. Jackman couldn't make out anyone giving chase.

Gasping for breath he leaned forward and clutched his knees, his eyes peeled for any signs of his assailant.

Nothing.

Satisfied that he had eluded his attacker, he wondered what to do next.

He decided to call his bank again. He needed cash. All he needed now was a phone—one with a secure land line. None was in sight. He wandered this way and that, searching.

He stepped onto the balcony and at last located a phone booth. They were few and far between these days, what with the proliferation of cell phones.

"I need money from my account," he told the customer service rep.

"Hello. I'm Claudia. You can't make any more withdrawals from an ATM today."

"I didn't make those withdrawals. How

much money do I have in my account?"

Claudia paused a beat. "Let's see. Yep, that's what it says."

"Says what? What are you babbling about?"

"I'm sorry to say you've got nothing in your account."

Jackman stood speechless. Then he managed a feeble "You must be wrong."

"No. You've got zero."

"I've been robbed!"

He grasped his forehead, breaking into a cold sweat.

"Who robbed you, sir?"

"I don't know."

"Do you know what he looks like?"

"He looks like me."

"A case of identity theft, you think?"

"I'm sure."

She confided to him, "They say if you see your double, it means you're going to die. You know, a doppelganger."

"Cheer me up, why don't you?"

"Right, sir. I know you're distraught. I'm just trying to help you."

"If this is your idea of help, I hope you never try to screw me."

"Settle down. Would you like to press charges against this doppelganger?"

At the end of his rope, he said, "Are you trying to be funny?"

"No, not at all. Do you want to press charges against him?"

"What do you think?"

"Fine. I'll mail the necessary documents to

your address and you can fill them out."

Jackman hung up. He dialed Kingsley's number.

The balcony on which he stood commanded a view of the Treasure Island Casino across the boulevard. Two make-believe pirate ships appeared to be floating in front of the casino.

Rocking back and forth the two ships exchanged shots. Firecrackers and gun smoke filled the sky above them. Women sailed in one ship, men the other. As the ships attacked each other, the crews sang and danced.

"Sir, our informant's been shot," Jackman told Kingsley over the phone line.

Jackman didn't use a mobile phone because its radio waves were easily monitored.

"What!" said Kingsley.

"Somebody killed him."

"Did you get a chance to talk to him before he was killed?"

"Yeah. Oswald was involved in a conspiracy with the Mafia to kill Kennedy, according to this guy."

"Who the hell killed our snitch? The mob?"

"I don't know. The killer tried to ice me too."

"Did the snitch have evidence supporting his accusations?"

"In his room safe."

"You need to get it."

"Hell."

"What's wrong?"

Jackman felt a hand on his shoulder. He half turned. An overweight cop was holding him.

"Yes, Officer," said Jackman.

Beyond the cop, he saw a woman gesticulating. She was pointing at him, jumping up and down, yelling, "That's him! He's the killer!"

"Would you come with me, sir?" the cop said courteously but forcibly.

"What's this all about?"

The cop glanced at the overwrought woman. "She says she saw you shoot a man in the restaurant downstairs."

"It wasn't me. That same killer tried to shoot me too."

"Please come with me, sir, so we can clear this up."

"I'm a federal agent," said Jackman. "I work for the CIA."

The cop eyed him skeptically with beady blue eyes, his puffy pink face looking distinctly porcine. "Do you have ID?"

"Talk to the man on the phone. He's my supervisor."

Jackman handed the phone receiver to the cop.

Grudgingly, the cop accepted it and spoke into it. "Hello. This man here says he's a CIA agent working for you."

Jackman breathed easier now, grateful that he had been talking to Kingsley at the time he was approached by the cop. "He'll vouch for me."

Standing twenty feet behind the accusing woman was the thief and probable killer, Jackman realized.

"There's the killer!" he told the cop. "Over there!"

The cop was still talking on the phone.

"Don't let him get away," Jackman told the cop.

The cop scratched his potbelly and offered the phone back to Jackman, who clutched it.

The cop said, "This guy on the phone says he works for the CIA."

"I know. I told you he's my supervisor."

"He says he never heard of you."

Jackman could not believe his ears. Was he losing his mind? he wondered.

"Sir, tell him the truth!" he blurted into the phone receiver.

Kingsley hung up.

Aghast, Jackman thought, *Plausible deniability*. Jackman was publicly involved in a murder, which would draw attention to the CIA's involvement in the crime. There was no way, he knew, that the Agency could acknowledge that he worked for them. Not now.

"The killer's over there," Jackman told the cop, looking past the cop's shoulder.

The cop turned to look behind him.

The thief, the stealer of Jackman's identity, seemed to laugh at Jackman then turned around and strode briskly away, losing himself in the crowd.

This couldn't be happening, Jackman decided. He must be imagining it. Or was he indeed slipping into madness? Was his unhinged mind conjuring up impossible chimeras?

The cop took hold of Jackman's wrist and with his other hand removed a pair of high-tensile steel handcuffs from his black leather belt.

"Sir, I'm placing you under arrest for

murder," said the cop as he slid the handcuff onto Jackman's wrist then locked it with a loud snick. "You have the right to an attorney—"

"You can't do this," protested Jackman. "I have evidence proving Lee Harvey Oswald was hired by a Mafia capo to assassinate JFK!"

The cop gazed at him with blank eyes.

"He's mad!" the woman who had pointed him out to the cop shrieked. She cringed. "He's stark raving mad! Psycho killer!"

The Counterfeit Man

"I didn't kill him," he said.

Brad Jackman sat in handcuffs and ankle irons on a less than comfortable couch in the Las Vegas prison psychiatrist's office. He wore a prisoner's orange jumpsuit.

The psychiatrist Dr. Frieda Shelton, sat in a chair opposite him, a notepad in one hand, a pen in the other.

Shelton, just turned forty, wore round black plastic glasses, which afforded her face an owl-like aspect. Her legs crossed, she wore a creme-de-menthe skirt that rode about two inches above her topmost knee.

"A witness says you did," she told Jackman.

"The killer was someone who looks like me."

Shelton hung fire. "Let's start at the beginning. What is your name?"

"Brad Jackman."

"What is your occupation?" she asked, taking notes.

"Is this confidential between you and me?"

"Yes. We have doctor/patient privilege."

"I'm a CIA hit man."

Shelton looked taken aback for a moment then recovered her composure. "That's an interesting line of work."

"Are you taping this conversation?"

"Does it matter?"

"It matters to me."

"Why?"

"I work for the CIA," he said, his patience wearing thin. "That's not something I want broadcast to the whole world."

"How do you expect me to help you if you don't talk to me?"

"I don't want your help. It wasn't my idea to come here. The cops sent me here."

She studied his face. "Can we proceed?"

"You didn't answer my question."

"What question?"

"Are you taping me?"

"I need to study your answers after our session."

"Turn off the tape recorder."

She didn't answer.

"I won't talk unless you turn if off," he said. He eyed the notepad in her hand. "You're already taking notes. You can study your notes after our 'session.'" He didn't like her use of the word *session*.

She thought for a moment, got up, crossed the room to her desk, opened the top drawer, and turned off the cassette recorder. She returned to her seat.

"OK," she said. "Let's start over. What do you do for a living?"

"I kill people for the CIA."

"Then you admit you killed a man in the Grand Lux Café at the Venetian Casino last night."

"No. I didn't kill *that* man."

"Then who did?"

"I told you. A guy that looks like me."

"Don't you think that's strange?"

"Don't you?"

She didn't answer him. "Did you actually see him kill the other man?"

Jackman hesitated. "No. I didn't see the killer."

"Then how do you know he looked like you?"

"I saw him robbing my bank account at an ATM earlier."

Shelton shook her head. "He robbed you then tried to kill you?"

"That's right."

"Why?"

"I don't know. I can guess."

"Yes . . . ?"

"He robbed me because he wanted money. He tried to waste me because Joe told me about the conspiracy. I know too much."

"Wait a minute. Joe?"

"The guy who was whacked."

"And what's this conspiracy you're talking about?"

Jackman sighed. He leaned forward toward her. "This is strictly confidential between you and me."

"Please continue."

"Do you agree to tell no one about what I'm

about to tell you?" he persisted.

"OK," she said as if it was no big deal, her eyes on her notepad.

"The mobster Sam Giancana hired Lee Harvey Oswald to assassinate JFK."

Nonplussed, Shelton simply stared at Jackman.

At last she said, "I find that hard to believe."

"Joe had proof."

"He gave it to you?"

"No. He didn't get a chance."

"Let me get this straight. You think you're the victim of a conspiracy."

"I said there was a conspiracy to kill JFK."

"And you've become involved in it."

"They tried to blow me away because I found out about the conspiracy."

"Who?"

"I don't know who's behind it. Joe said there's a bigwig DC politician involved in the cover-up of the conspiracy."

Shelton leaned back in her chair. "Think about it, Brad. Why would anybody really want to kill you? You're a very small fish in a very big sea."

"I told you, I work for the CIA. That in itself makes me a target."

"That's not how I see it."

"What?" said Jackman, puzzled.

"As I see it, your occupation is an insurance salesman."

Jackman nodded. "That's my cover story. We call it a 'legend' in the Agency. How did you find that out?"

"Lieutenant Buco of the Las Vegas Police found your insurance adjuster's ID card in your wallet after they arrested you. He called your insurance agency boss, who confirmed it."

"My insurance boss works for the CIA too. That's his job—to confirm my legend."

"You sure know a lot of people who work for the CIA," she said incredulously.

"What's that supposed to mean?"

She switched tack. "Lieutenant Buco doesn't believe your claims that you work for the CIA. In fact, he thinks you're psychotic. That's why he sent you to me."

"Talk to my supervisor at the CIA if you don't believe me."

"Lieutenant Buco already did that. Your so-called CIA supervisor said he never heard of you."

Jackman nodded. "He can't admit it. That would blow my cover."

"Did you ever hear of Walter Mitty?"

"What are you trying to say?" said Jackman, barely restraining his irritation.

"Walter Mitty imagined he was all kinds of heroes. In fact, he was nothing of the sort. He was anything but."

"A short-story character lives in a dreamworld. So?"

"Isn't it possible, Brad, that you're imagining your job as a hit man for the CIA?"

"You've got to be kidding. What kind of dime-store psychobabble is this?"

"If you really work for the CIA, how come nobody will confirm it?"

"Plausible deniability," he shot back.

She made a show of turning the page in her notepad. "Let's move on. Now, you said you're a hit man."

"Right."

"Don't you feel any guilt for murdering people?"

"No. Should I? It's my job."

"Frankly, yes, you should."

"Don't you feel any guilt for picking apart your patients' minds?"

"I psychoanalyze them to help them."

"I kill enemies of our country to save our country."

She cleared her throat politely. "Let's move on," she said.

"Fine."

"Do you have a girlfriend, Brad?"

"What's that got to do with anything?"

"Does my question bother you?"

"Your question is immaterial."

"Let me be the judge of that. Well, do you?"

"No. It's hard to keep a girlfriend in my line of work."

"So you've invented your occupation as a CIA agent to attract women?"

Jackman shook his head in frustration at her inability to accept the truth. "No."

"Don't you like girls?" she coaxed.

"Yeah."

"You're not gay, are you?"

"No."

"To impress women you tell them you're a spy."

He threw up his hands in disgust, as well as he could with handcuffs on them, anyway. "That's right. How'd you guess? I have an insatiable appetite for women," he said, his lips dripping with sarcasm, "so I pretend I'm a hit man for the CIA."

She shifted her legs, lifting her top right leg, uncrossed them, and recrossed them in the opposite order, right leg bottommost, exposing a lot of creamy white thigh along the way.

Wait a minute, he thought. *Is she coming on to me?*

She fastened the top button on her chartreuse sateen blouse. "If you like women, why don't you have a girlfriend?"

"How did we get on this subject?"

"Answer the question, please."

"I'm too busy with my work to spend time chasing skirts."

"You should make time—"

Shelton's cell phone beeped.

"Excuse me," she said. She withdrew her mobile from her purse, answered it.

"Yes," she said into the receiver. She listened. After a while she said, "OK," and ended the call.

She stood up. "You'll have to excuse me." She headed for another office. "I'll be back after I take this call." She shut the door behind her.

The phone on the desk rang. Jackman started. He decided to answer it—which wasn't easy given his handcuffs. The ankle irons didn't help any either.

He shambled toward the desk, managed to lift the handset to his ear, and said hello.

He heard a click. Nothing else. That was that. *Strange*, he thought. It gave him the creeps.

He hung up.

He returned to the couch.

The door to the hallway opened. A man bolted into the patient office. It was the guy that looked like Jackman. The killer. He had a wild look on his face. He spotted Jackman on the couch.

"Don't talk or I'll kill you," he told Jackman, rushed him, and rammed his fist into Jackman's stomach with all his might.

Jackman, who was recumbent, gasped and doubled over, clutching his throbbing stomach, breaking into a sweat. The guy knew how to throw a punch, Jackman decided, wincing among waves of pain.

Jackman's spitting image made a beeline for the door and darted into the hallway.

Jackman tried to get to his feet to give pursuit, but the pain in his gut got the better of him. He stumbled over his ankle irons and fell to his knees, groaning.

Shelton entered the room from her private office, twigged Jackman's predicament, and bustled to his aid.

"Are you ill?" she asked. "What's wrong?"

With her help, Jackman rose to his feet and said, "He attacked me."

"Who?"

"The guy who's impersonating me."

Shelton quartered the room. "I don't see anyone."

"He took off."

Shelton helped Jackman to the couch, made

for the hallway door, cracked it, and peered down the corridor. Moments later she shut the door.

"There's nobody out there," she said.

"He was here, I tell you."

"What did he want?"

"He threatened to kill me if I talked."

"I didn't hear anything from my office."

Jackman's eyes lit up. "Turn on the tape recorder! You'll hear his voice."

She headed for her desk, balked, and said, "Don't you remember? You told me to switch it off."

"Damn," he muttered.

She scrutinized his face. "If he attacked you like you say he did, where's the bruise?"

"He didn't hit my face. He punched me in the stomach."

"Do you feel better now?"

"Yeah."

He relaxed on the couch, tried to, in any case. Relaxing in handcuffs and ankle irons wasn't the easiest thing, he decided.

"All right," she said, sitting on her chair and picking up her notepad and pen. "Where were we?"

"I'm being framed," he said.

"For what?"

"For Joe's murder."

"By whom?"

"I don't know for sure. Probably someone who's in on the conspiracy."

"The conspiracy against you?"

"The conspiracy that got Kennedy killed," he corrected her with more than a trace of ire, sensing mockery in her tone.

"But why? Why frame you?"

He stared at his hands on his lap. "I don't know," he said under his breath.

"Does that make sense to you?"

"What?"

"That somebody would want to frame you for a murder?"

"Yeah—if they wanted me out of the picture."

"Out of the picture?"

"Out of the cover-up of the conspiracy. I can blow the lid off it with the inside skinny Joe gave me."

"You have no evidence corroborating your claims."

"It's in Joe's hotel room safe—if somebody would just go there and get it."

"Calm down, Brad. I'm trying to help you."

"Help me what?" he demanded.

"Help you see you're suffering from delusions. Think of what you're saying—"

At that moment, the front door burst open.

Two men over six feet tall clad in dark suits, a gimpy redhead and a brunette with somber expressions on their faces, charged in, automatics in hands. The men wore ear buds with tan coiled wires trailing down their necks and under the backs of their jackets.

To Jackman's trained eye the automatics looked like Beretta Tomcats that used .32 ACP loads in seven-round clips.

Bowled over, Shelton gazed in awe at the two intruders, her mouth falling open.

Recovering her equanimity to a degree, she

said, "Who the hell are you?"

"CIA agents," said the redhead, pulled ID out of his breast pocket, and flashed it in front of her.

"You don't need guns in here, gentlemen," said Shelton. "Tell me what you want before I call the police."

"You'll do no such thing," said the gimpy redhead.

White-faced with indignation, Shelton stared at him.

"He's wanted by the Agency," said Brunette, the more dour of the two agents.

"For what?" asked Shelton.

"He's an impostor. He's impersonating a CIA agent. We'll take care of him."

"I'll call the police," said Shelton. "Let them handle it."

"We don't want the police involved. This is a national security matter."

Brunette helped Jackman roughly to his feet.

"What are you talking about?" cried Jackman, struggling to escape Brunette's grip. "I'm not the impostor!"

"This man's a paranoid schizophrenic," said Shelton. "He thinks conspirators are out to get him."

"I'm not the impostor!" rapped out Jackman. "The impostor killed Joe."

"Let's go," the gimpy redhead told Jackman and together with Brunette shepherded him out of the police psychiatrist's office into the hallway and shut the door behind them.

Once in the corridor, the gimpy redhead said

to the squirming prisoner, "What's this all about, Jackman?" and let go of him.

Startled, Jackman said, "You know I'm Jackman?"

"Yeah, yeah. Kingsley sent us."

"I thought he hung me out to dry . . . ," Jackman trailed off.

"So, what gives?"

"My impostor wasted our informant."

"That's what this is all about?"

"I told Kingsley everything over the phone."

"How the hell did you get into this mess, Jackman?"

Jackman held up his shackled hands. "Get me out of these."

The gimpy redhead grabbed Jackman's elbow and hustled him forward. "We've got to get out of here before the Vegas cops come. That shrink's probably calling them right now."

Somebody stepped out of the elevator in front of them.

It was Jackman's impostor, Jackman realized.

A silenced automatic in his gloved hand, the double opened fire on them and cut down the two CIA agents with two head shots in a matter of seconds.

"Why you!" cried Jackman and clenched his right fist, failing to realize that his double could just as easily shoot him to boot.

His double snickered and ducked back into the elevator.

Fighting his handcuffs Jackman scooped up the gimpy redhead's Beretta with difficulty, fumbling it in his haste, and gave chase, but stumbled over his ankle irons, ruining any kind of a shot.

His double gloated at him and tossed over the silenced automatic in his direction. The gun clattered to the floor. The elevator door wheezed shut.

"Who are you?" Jackman yelled after him.

Shelton entered the corridor from her office.

She screamed when she spotted the blood-soaked bodies crumpled on the grey linoleum floor beside Jackman.

"What have you done, Brad!"

Zoltana

"You're not impressing me," Shelton told Jackman as they sat in the Deuce double-decker bus driving down Las Vegas Boulevard.

"What are you talking about?" said Jackman. He held the silenced automatic between his legs.

"You're pretending to be a CIA hit man to impress me, aren't you?"

Jackman shook his head wearily. "Why do I want to impress you?"

"You tell women you're a CIA agent to impress them and then bed them. I'm not impressed."

"I *am* a CIA hit man."

"You're pretending to be one, Brad. You think CIA hit men impress women."

"I could care less about impressing you. You're the one who asked me in your office what I did for a living. And I told you."

"Your fantasies are taking over your life, Brad. You need to accept the fact that they are, in fact, fantasies."

"The gun in my hand isn't a fantasy." He waved the silenced automatic between his legs. "The guy who looks like me and is trying to kill me isn't a fantasy either."

"But he is, Brad."

"He killed those two CIA agents in the police station."

"No, Brad. You did. You're suffering from schizophrenia. Your girlfriend dumped you and you're withdrawing from reality by pretending to be a CIA agent."

"*Cherchez la femme,* huh?" He smiled ironically to himself.

"I can help you. You need treatment."

"I need to kill that son-of-a-bitch lookalike who wasted Joe and tried to waste me."

"There is no lookalike, Brad. Don't you see?"

"Cut out the psychobabble and maybe, just maybe, this bus ride will be bearable."

"Where are we going?"

"We're escaping the killer. Haven't you been paying attention?"

"But you're the killer. You killed those two CIA agents."

"The guy who looks like me did that." Jackman shook his head in frustration.

The bus stopped in front of Caesar's Palace to allow passengers to disembark.

A middle-aged woman was scolding her boy in the seat in front of Jackman's. There was another kid behind Jackman. Jackman could feel him kicking the back of his seat.

"Let's get out of here," Jackman told Shelton. "I think we've lost him by now."

"That wouldn't be hard," she said wearily.

Jackman turned on her. "What do you mean by that?"

"What do you think? Nobody's chasing us—yet."

He gave her a look.

"The cops . . . ," she said, nodding.

The other passengers were gabbling raucously, speaking in different tongues. They hailed from all parts of the world and descended on Las Vegas like a swarm of frenzied locusts bent on denuding Vegas of its money—except that they themselves would more than likely be the ones denuded.

The kid stitting behind him launched a particularly hard kick against Jackman's seat-back that caused the whole seat to shudder.

"Enough!" said Jackman, grabbed Shelton's wrist, and made for the bus exit.

They walked by the Mirage's waterfalls and angled toward Caesar's Palace. They pulled up at the door to the Forum shops.

Jackman glanced behind him to make sure nobody was following them. He cast around a bit, saw no one conspicuous, then, relaxing, opened the heavy plate-glass door to the shops.

A large rectangular pool stretched before him.

He and Shelton ascended two flights of steps to the third floor. They strolled down the corridor window-shopping at the boutiques to their right and left.

They entered a central concourse where a large white statue of a herd of stallions stood in a fountain.

Above the shops, highlighted by the faux cerulean sky of the cathedral ceiling, white statues of ancient Roman soldiers stood seemingly on guard over both the grounds and the customers below.

Jackman led Shelton into a fortune-teller's small office shoehorned between two ritzy boutiques.

Pictures of three-foot-high Tarot cards lined the interior walls. Jasmine incense permeated the air.

Jackman parted a curtain of alternating brown and orange wooden beads with his hand and entered the main room as the beads rattled around him.

A wild-eyed gypsy woman reeking of patchouli sat at a small round table. Her large black eyes that looked like nothing so much as pupils without irides registered Jackman's presence with a shade of interest. Jackman wanted to gag on the patchouli.

"What are we doing here?" Shelton asked Jackman.

"I've never been in one of these places."

"Please sit down," the gypsy told Jackman, "and I will tell you your future."

Her long raven hair was as black as her humongous liquid eyes.

"Are you a gypsy?" he asked her, sitting down.

"Actually I am from Guatemala. My family has the gift of foresight."

"It doesn't surprise me," said Shelton, standing at Jackman's side, a look of amused cynicism hijacking her face.

"My name is Zoltana," said the fortune-teller, ignoring Shelton's remark.

"I wish you'd just turn yourself in to the police," Shelton told Jackman.

He silenced her with a glance.

Zoltana weighed Shelton's words but kept her own counsel.

Zoltana paused a beat. Then, "Do you wish to proceed?" she asked Jackman.

"No," said Shelton. "We do not. This is superstitious mumbo-jumbo."

"Yeah," Jackman told Zoltana. "Let's proceed."

Shelton sighed and shook her head in disgust.

"Hold your left palm before you over the tabletop," Zoltana instructed Jackman.

Shelton was staring at him through her round black plastic glasses that gave her face an owl-like aspect. He expected her to hoot any second.

She unnerved him looking at him so smugly. He didn't let it show. He extended his hand palm-up toward Zoltana.

Taking it in her hand she examined it underneath the overhead light.

"A great man once said, 'Character is destiny,'" she said. "I can't really see the future, but I can reveal your character to you. And your character is what will mold your future."

"Hogwash," muttered Shelton.

"Don't mind her," Jackman told Zoltana. "She's a psychiatrist."

Zoltana nodded, as if to say that explained it. She perused his palm.

"You have an overactive imagination," she said at last.

"Maybe there's something to this after all," chipped in Shelton.

"Do you mind?" Jackman rebuked her.

Zoltana frowned at his palm.

"What is it?" asked Jackman. "What do you see? I want to know."

"Very well. Your future is fraught with peril. You have enemies. Your profession . . . ," she trailed off.

"Yes," he encouraged her. "My profession?"

"Your profession leads you into contact with people who might want to harm you."

"Do I have a doppelganger?" he blurted.

She scrutinized his palm. "It's strange that you should ask that. Yes, you do. He will try to hurt you."

"Oh come on," scoffed Shelton.

Jackman waved her off. "Will he succeed?" he asked Zoltana, on the edge of his seat.

"That's up to you. I told you, I can't see the future. I can see possibilities, one of which will ultimately transpire on account of your character."

"This gobbledygook is going too far," said Shelton.

"You yourself may have the gift," Zoltana told Jackman.

"What gift?" he asked.

"Second sight. The ability to see more than others can. To see beyond reality as others see it. To see your doppelganger."

"Then there are such things as doppelgangers?"

"Of course."

"Of course," mimicked Shelton. "*Not.*"

"That'll be a hundred dollars," Zoltana told Jackman, letting go of his hand.

Shelton burst out laughing.

Jackman reached for his wallet. "Is it true that if you see your doppelganger, it means you're gonna die?"

He handed her five twenty-dollar bills.

"Yes," she said.

"Poppycock," scoffed Shelton.

"Does that mean I'm gonna die?" he asked Zoltana.

She delayed her reply. To Jackman it looked as if she was struggling with herself trying to figure out how to answer. In the end she said, "I don't know."

"You do know," he said, pouncing on her.

"No, I don't." She gathered the twenties in her hands as if adjusting a bouquet of roses. "That's all I know."

"Why won't you tell me?"

"I've told you everything I know. That's all I know," she said, her eyes avoiding his, hastening her movements gathering herself.

"Let's leave, Brad," said Shelton. "This is nothing but an act."

"She knows, I tell you," he said.

"She doesn't know anything. She told you what you wanted to hear. That's how these so-called palmists and fortune-tellers operate."

"I must retire now," said Zoltana and left the room.

Jackman and Shelton emerged from the fortune-teller parlor onto the concourse.

"The best thing for you to do, Brad, is to turn yourself in to the police for those two murders of the CIA agents."

Jackman was growing weary of telling her again and again, but he said anyway, "I didn't plug them. My double—"

"Not that tired story," she interrupted in exasperation.

"Let's drop it."

"I feel uncomfortable being with a murderer. I want to go home."

He fixed his eyes on her. "No way. You might go to the cops about me. I can't risk that."

"I'll scream."

He grabbed her elbow and pressed the silenced muzzle of his automatic against her side, digging it through the fabric of his racing jacket's pocket, goading her soft stomach flesh with the steel.

"Then I'll have to kill you," he said coolly.

Something like fear and annoyance registered in her eyes.

"Scaring a woman isn't the way to her heart," she said.

"Do you still think I'm doing all this in order to seduce you?"

"You need professional help, Brad. You're crying out for it."

They walked near the fountain containing the majestic horses. It roared in their ears, spraying them with cool drops from the gushing water. Knots of tourists stood around the fountain, snapping pictures of their friends and families who posed in front of it.

Jackman sensed something bad was going to happen. He felt it in his bones. The feeling wouldn't go away.

www.ingramcontent.com/pod-product-compliance
Lightning Source LLC
Chambersburg PA
CBHW022134240626
47153CB00007B/2364